FROM THE NANCY DREW FILES

THE CASE: The jockey set to ride the favorite in the Kentucky Derby takes a nasty spill that may not have been accidental.

CONTACT: Nancy's father, Carson Drew, has a share in a Derby horse called Pied Piper.

SUSPECTS: Cameron Parker—*the handsome trainer might be racing from his dark past.*

Ace Hanford—*a jockey who runs in the fast lane.*

Dollar Bill—*the bookie with an unpleasant payment policy.*

COMPLICATIONS: A prowler has been trying to get to the Derby horses at night—*including Pied Piper!*

D0089174

Books in The Nancy Drew Files™ Series

Available from ARCHWAY Paperbacks

THE NANCY DREW FILES™ CASE · 46

WIN, PLACE OR DIE

Carolyn Keene

PB
KEE

AN ARCHWAY PAPERBACK
Published by POCKET BOOKS
New York   London   Toronto   Sydney   Tokyo   Singapore

AN ARCHWAY PAPERBACK *Original*

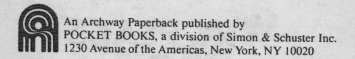

An Archway Paperback published by
POCKET BOOKS, a division of Simon & Schuster Inc.
1230 Avenue of the Americas, New York, NY 10020

Copyright © 1990 by Simon & Schuster Inc.
Cover art copyright © 1990 Jim Mathewuse
Produced by Mega-Books of New York, Inc.

ISBN: 0-671-67498-6

First Archway Paperback printing April 1990

10 9 8 7 6 5 4 3 2 1

NANCY DREW, AN ARCHWAY PAPERBACK and colophon are registered trademarks of Simon & Schuster Inc.

THE NANCY DREW FILES is a trademark of Simon & Schuster Inc.

Printed in the U.S.A.

IL 7+

WIN, PLACE OR DIE

Chapter

One

BORED, BORED, BORED!" Nancy Drew said, picking up a news magazine. She thumbed through it, tossed it aside, and flopped down on the living room sofa. "I'm bored!"

The girl detective stared at the ceiling, listening to the rain that had plagued River Heights all week. She'd had to cancel her tennis lesson that afternoon, and unless the weather broke soon, her match that weekend would have to be postponed, too. Tapping her foot on the sofa's armrest, she checked her watch. Bess Marvin had promised to stop by around five o'clock, after her hair appointment, but it was already almost six.

Hearing the back door open, Nancy jumped to her feet. "Dad? Is that you?"

"Yes, Nan," Carson Drew, River Heights's famous criminal lawyer, called out.

Nancy hurried into the kitchen, where her father was just laying his briefcase and the evening paper on the table. "Am I glad you're home. I've had the dullest day in history! Hannah's visiting friends, George is on that trip with her parents, and Bess is almost an hour late!"

Her father laughed and gave her a quick hug. "And you don't have a mystery to occupy your time." He paused. "I think I may have a cure."

Nancy's detective instincts went on red alert. During the course of his work, her father stumbled on many mysteries. Maybe he'd found one now.

Carson unfolded the newspaper to the sports section. Above a black-and-white photo of horses thundering down a racetrack, the headline read: "Top Three-Year-Olds Ready to Run for the Roses." Beneath that, in smaller letters, it stated: "Derby Crowd Expected to Be Largest Ever."

Nancy glanced at her father quizzically. "The Kentucky Derby?"

"The greatest two minutes in sports," her father added. "Now that we're owners of Pied Piper—" he started to say, pointing to the horse in the center of the field.

Nancy stared at her father, amazed. "What do you mean we own a racehorse?" she interrupted.

Carson Drew's handsome face broke into a smile. "I just bought into a three-year-old Thoroughbred with some business associates of mine. We now own a quarter share of Pied Piper."

"You're kidding!" Nancy's blue eyes sparkled with excitement. "Dad, that's great! Does Pied Piper have a chance of winning the Derby?"

"Well, I certainly hope so. Thea Rodriguez, the colt's trainer, seems to have confidence in him."

"Pied Piper's trainer is a woman?" Nancy asked.

Carson nodded. "One of the best in the business, I understand."

"Wow!" Nancy quickly scanned the article. "When exactly is the Derby?"

"A week from tomorrow—Saturday." Carson frowned. "I'd like to go, but a case I've been working on is scheduled for trial next week. I'm afraid I can't make it."

"Oh, Dad. That's lousy!"

Carson grimaced. "It certainly is. Someone will have to go and watch out for my interests."

"One of the other owners?" Nancy guessed.

"Unfortunately, all of the owners have commitments they can't break," he said regretfully.

"Okay, I'll bite. Who?" Nancy's blue eyes

danced at the teasing smile that spread across her father's lips. "Not me?"

"If you're not too busy."

"Busy! Dad, this is great!" She flung her arms around his neck as the front bell pealed loudly. "That's Bess!" Nancy cried. "Could I ask her to go along with me?"

Carson laughed. "Ask away. In fact, I'd be happy to know you had a friend with you."

Nancy raced to the door. Bess, her blond hair trimmed and freshly styled, stood on the porch. Before Nancy could tell her the good news, Bess wailed, "My hair! Look at my hair! No, don't look at it!" She tried to cover up the front of it.

Nancy's brows lifted. "What's wrong? Your hair looks great!"

"The front!" Bess moaned. "She cut bangs and she cut them too short—they're all jagged and weird. The whole haircut makes me look like a Fashion Don't!"

"Oh, come on. It can't be that bad." Nancy pulled Bess's hands from her forehead. "You look terrific. The bangs are fine. No problem."

"You really think so?" Bess asked doubtfully.

"Would I lie to you?" Nancy answered. "Come on. Forget about your hair for a minute. I've got tons to tell you."

She led Bess into the den and then quickly

filled her in on the Kentucky Derby and Pied
Piper.

"Your dad owns a Thoroughbred and wants us
to go to Louisville?" Bess repeated when Nancy
finished. "Oh, I can't wait!" She paced the den
floor, muttering under her breath. "I've got to
convince Mom and Dad, and I've got to go
shopping. But this hair!" She closed her eyes in
remembered misery.

"I can see you two have a lot to talk about,"
Nancy's father said dryly, standing in the den
doorway. "I wrote Thea's hotel number on the
pad by the kitchen phone. I left word you'd get in
touch with her tonight. There's a hotel reserva-
tion waiting for you, too. One of my partners
made it months ago. Since he can't go, it's all
yours."

"Let's call her," Nancy suggested after her dad
left.

"Right after I talk to my parents," Bess agreed.

Although it took a little convincing, Mr. and
Mrs. Marvin agreed to let Bess go with Nancy.
Bess whooped with delight when she replaced the
receiver.

Next Nancy phoned Thea Rodriguez, but the
trainer wasn't in her room. Nancy left a message
saying she and a friend would be arriving in
Louisville sometime Monday afternoon. "I'd

better make the flight reservations right now," she added, grabbing the phone book.

Thirty minutes later all their plans were set. "I can't believe it!" Bess said before she left the Drews' later that evening.

"Well, start believing it." Nancy grinned. "Early Monday morning, we're heading for the Kentucky Derby!"

As soon as their flight landed in Louisville, Nancy's pulse began to pound wildly. She and Bess picked up their bright red rental car and drove through Louisville's busy pre-Derby streets to their downtown hotel. Hurriedly they changed into shorts and light cotton blouses. It was only a little after one when they were on their way to Churchill Downs, the famous racetrack of the Kentucky Derby.

Bess adjusted the baseball cap she'd stuck on her head to cover her bangs. "Look, Nancy!" she cried excitedly. "We're almost there!"

Nancy glanced through the windshield. In the distance the twin spires on top of the grandstand were etched against a powder blue sky. "Just a few more minutes," Nancy agreed. "I can't wait to meet Thea. She said she'd be with Pied Piper at the barn ten."

"What did she sound like?" Bess asked.

"Nice. Busy though. We barely had a chance to

talk. She spends practically every minute with Pied Piper." Nancy pulled to a stop at a red light. "She told me she even sleeps on a cot in the barn most nights, so she can be near him."

Nancy parked as near as she could to the wire fence that surrounded the stable area. Horse trailers were everywhere. According to the pamphlet she'd picked up at her hotel, Derby hopefuls weren't the only horses housed in the barns. Other Thoroughbreds slotted for races run earlier in the week were also stabled there.

Although it was only about ten miles from Louisville to Churchill Downs, Nancy noticed the carnival atmosphere of the city had disappeared. The mood was subdued by the racetrack stable area. Race people obviously took their sport seriously.

"Which one is barn ten?" Bess wondered out loud, glancing around at the row of buildings.

Nancy studied the numerous buildings and shrugged. "Let's ask."

They passed through a narrow gate. Ahead lay the brown ribbon of track as it swept one and a quarter miles in front of the sheds, barns, grandstand, clubhouse, and bleachers.

"Wow," Bess said, awestruck by the scene in front of her.

The place was busy with people and horses, alive with noise and the sharp scent of the

7

Thoroughbreds. "Maybe we should go to the secretary's office," Nancy said, remembering Thea had said that was where everyone checked in.

"Wait a minute," said Bess. "Here comes somebody. Do you think he's a jockey?"

The short, red-haired man heading their way could easily be a jockey, Nancy decided. She knew all Derby horses carried one hundred twenty-six pounds during the race. The jockey had to weigh even less because the saddle accounted for some of the weight. The guy coming toward them looked about a hundred and ten and was several inches shorter than Nancy.

Nancy smiled in greeting, but just before he reached them, the redhead turned toward the fence near the track, digging into the pocket of his jacket. He pulled out a piece of paper and scowled down at it.

"He doesn't look like he's in a good mood, does he?" Bess murmured.

Tucking a strand of reddish blond hair behind her ear, Nancy wrinkled her nose. "Not exactly. Let's find someone else to ask."

They had taken only two steps when a heavyset older man with a flattened nose marched straight toward them and almost collided with Bess. Bess stopped short, and the man brushed past her, bumping against her shoulder. He strode straight for the red-haired jockey without a word of apology.

"Well, excuse me," Bess muttered under her breath.

"He doesn't look like he's in a good mood, either," Nancy remarked. The jockey started yelling at the heavyset man as soon as he joined him.

"I said I'd get you your money, didn't I? Now leave me alone!" the jockey shouted.

The older man snapped back an answer in a low voice, too soft for Nancy to hear. Intrigued, Nancy eased back a few steps, pulling Bess with her.

"What are you doing?" Bess whispered in her ear.

"Shhh—I'm listening."

The jockey was glaring at the older man, his face ghostly white. Nancy leaned close to Bess, pretending to talk to her. In reality her attention was on the two men.

"I'm not stiffing," the jockey asserted, his voice lower now but shaking with emotion. "You'll get your money the right way!"

The man with the flattened nose suddenly glanced over his shoulder. His dark scowl centered on Nancy.

Nancy's heart lurched. Heaving a deep sigh, she complained dramatically, "Oh, I don't know,

Bess. It's all a little disappointing, don't you think?"

Bess gazed at her in blank disbelief. "Well, sure," she said slowly. "I mean, I guess so." She leaned closer and whispered, "Are you serious?"

"Of course not," Nancy whispered back through a plastered-on smile. Something strange was going on between the jockey and the heavyset man, and she was going to find out what.

The heavyset man, apparently reassured, turned back to the jockey. This time she caught the words he whispered to his friend. They sent a chill down her spine.

"By race day, McHugh," he growled in a raspy, threatening voice. "Or you can kiss more than the Derby goodbye!"

Chapter

Two

BEFORE NANCY COULD HEAR another word, the two men moved out of earshot. She did notice, though, that McHugh had turned even whiter at the other man's words.

"What was that all about?" Bess asked.

Nancy shook her head thoughtfully. "I don't know, but it sure sounded like a threat to me. What did you think?"

Bess rolled her eyes. "You're not trying to scare up a mystery by any chance, are you?"

"Maybe," Nancy admitted, her blue eyes twinkling. "It has been a while between cases." She glanced at the two retreating figures. "I just wish I knew what they were talking about."

She and Bess asked directions to the barns. As they peeked in one they could see a long row of stalls. The smell of horses and hay and feed hung in the dust-filled air. Pawing hooves, soft nickers, and snorts mingled with the shouts of stable boys. All contributed to the constant din.

As they approached barn ten, they heard a voice on the loudspeaker announce that the afternoon races would begin soon.

Barn ten was a beehive of activity. Grooms, stable boys, and trainers surrounded each horse.

"Which one is Pied Piper?" Bess asked as they walked in front of the stalls. "Do you think Thea will know us?"

"She told me she'd be—"

"Nancy Drew?" a woman's voice called out.

"—looking for me," Nancy finished, smiling at the young, trim, dark-haired woman approaching them.

"Thea Rodriguez." The trainer introduced herself, shaking Nancy's and Bess's hand in turn. Nancy liked the no-nonsense appeal of Thea's jeans and plaid work shirt. "I've been waiting for you. Wait till you see him. Pied Piper's the best horse I've ever trained!"

With no further introduction she led Bess and

Nancy toward Pied Piper's stall. The colt looked at them over the top of the gate, his tail switching nervously. The gloss of his fiery chestnut coat indicated he was well cared for. An off-center white star was nearly hidden by his forelock. As if sensing they were admiring him, he suddenly tossed his head and nickered.

"He's beautiful," Nancy said, feeling more than a little proud.

"Oh, I hope he wins," Bess said fervently. "Wouldn't that be the best?"

"It certainly would," Thea answered, her serious face breaking into a grin. "There are a lot of terrific horse races that a champion colt, or filly, can enter, but there's only one Derby. And only one chance to win it."

"What do you mean?" asked Bess.

"The Derby's only for three-year-olds," Thea explained, "so a horse can enter it only once."

"How did you become interested in being a trainer?" Nancy asked.

"My father was a trainer. A really good trainer," Thea added honestly. "I've been around horses all my life, and because my father was respected, the Thoroughbred owners respected me, too." She rubbed her hand down Pied Piper's long, silky nose. "When my father died, I wanted to take up where he'd left off, but it hasn't been as easy as I'd hoped. This is mainly a man's profession still. Some people don't think a woman can do the job."

"I know what you mean," Nancy said with feeling. "I have a similar problem sometimes."

"Your father told me you're a detective," Thea responded. "I'd like to hear about your cases sometime."

"Nancy's the best," Bess put in loyally as a short, wiry young man walked up to Thea.

"This is Jimmy Harris," Thea said, introducing them all. "Pied Piper's jockey."

"I'm heading out to the races now," he told Thea after saying hello to the girls. "Unless you need anything else."

Thea shook her head, and Jimmy gave Nancy and Bess a friendly smile before he left. He reminded Nancy of the red-haired jockey she'd seen earlier. She found herself wondering again what his quarrel with the heavyset man had been.

Nancy asked casually, "Is there a red-haired jockey here named McHugh?"

Thea glanced at Nancy with a worried frown. "McHugh rides for Johnson Farms. He's Toot Sweet's jockey in the Derby. Toot Sweet is the favorite."

"Toot Sweet is the horse's name?" Bess asked.

Nancy smiled. "In French *tout de suite* means

'right away.' Is that why the horse is named Toot Sweet?"

"Exactly," said Thea. "Apparently when Toot Sweet was a foal someone said, 'That little filly really moves across the field *tout de suite.'* So they named her Toot Sweet."

"Her?" Nancy repeated in surprise. "A filly's the favorite? Isn't that unusual?"

"Very," Thea agreed. "I see you've done some research," she added, obviously impressed. "Only two fillies have ever won the Derby— Regret back in 1915, and Genuine Risk in 1980. The colts are generally bigger and stronger. But Toot Sweet's a hefty girl."

Out of the corner of her eye Nancy caught sight of a handsome man in his early twenties moving their way. His blue denim work shirt set off piercing blue eyes and the balmy breeze ruffled his midnight black hair. He wore jeans, like Thea, and he walked with an easy gait that suggested he was part of the horse-racing scene.

"Well, here's the man to ask," Thea said, a smile finding its way to her lips. "Cameron Parker, I'd like you to meet Nancy Drew and her friend—"

"Bess Marvin," said Bess, staring at Parker with stars in her eyes. Trust Bess to zero in on the one sensational-looking guy around, Nancy thought, amused.

"Cam is Toot Sweet's trainer," Thea added. Her eyes met Cam's and held steady on them for a minute.

"So you're with Johnson Farms, too," Nancy said. "We saw Toot Sweet's jockey a little while ago."

Cam's dark brows pulled together in a frown. "Where?" he asked tersely.

"Standing by the stable area fence near the racecourse." Cam's reaction heightened Nancy's curiosity. "He was talking to a heavyset man with a flattened nose."

Cam's blue eyes turned wintry. "Was he?" he asked, his tone making it clear he wasn't happy. "Ken's supposed to be getting ready for Toot Sweet's public workout between races" was all he said, however. Turning to Thea, he added, "I just came to ask you if you'd like to see her run."

"In just a minute," Thea agreed. In a little while she invited Nancy and Bess to join them. "The public workouts are so people at the track can see the Derby horses in action. Toot Sweet's time will be announced over the loudspeaker. Let's go check out the competition," she said, swinging into motion.

On the way to the dirt track, Cam said to Nancy and Bess, "Thea and I pay close attention to all the horses and what they're doing. It's all

16

part of the business. It's better to get the facts from the horse's mouth, so to speak, than from some misinformed stable boy or racing enthusiast."

Nancy doubted that was the only reason Cam and Thea paid so much attention to each other, but she kept her thoughts to herself.

"There they are," Cam said as he, Thea, Nancy, and Bess circled the single wooden rail surrounding the track. Cam pointed at the stunning black filly that was thundering toward the backstretch. She was rapidly approaching the area where they were all standing, her strides eating up the turf. Nancy recognized the redheaded jockey sitting high in the saddle astride her.

Toot Sweet's muscles gleamed like oiled satin. She looked tough and fit and a match for any of the colts that would be running against her on Derby day.

"Wow," Bess said, taking a step backward as Toot Sweet swept around the curve, turf kicking up from behind her flashing hooves. Even though the rail separated them from the track, Bess obviously wasn't taking any chances.

"She looks terrific, Cam," Thea murmured appreciatively, stepping close to him and away from the girls.

Toot Sweet charged forward, moving toward

them. An extra movement beneath her belly suddenly caught Nancy's eye. The girth had come undone!

"The saddle!" Nancy cried, pointing.

At that moment McHugh pitched forward on Toot Sweet's neck. Confused, the Thoroughbred pulled sharply to the right, tearing straight toward them.

Bess screamed. Nancy stepped back in horror. A thousand pounds of thundering Thoroughbred was charging out of control. Toot Sweet was about to crash through the rail—straight at Bess and Nancy.

Chapter

Three

Nancy dove to the right, pulling Bess with her. Inches from the rail the horse twisted and reared. McHugh and the saddle slid off her back and landed hard in the packed dirt. Frightened, Toot Sweet bolted, zigzagging around the track.

Nancy picked herself up off the ground and helped Bess to her feet. Cam vaulted the rail to help McHugh, who was still lying on the ground.

"Oh, Nancy. What happened?" Bess asked, her voice shaking.

"I don't know," Nancy said grimly, climbing over the rail to help Cam.

Thea and Bess were on her heels. "I'll catch Toot Sweet before she hurts herself," Thea said.

When Nancy reached Ken McHugh, the jockey was struggling to his feet and dusting himself off.

"What happened?" Cam asked furiously, not bothering to ask if McHugh was all right. "Toot Sweet could have injured herself and you, too!"

"Well, it wasn't my fault!" McHugh snapped back. "The saddle slipped and the horse went crazy!"

"Why wasn't the saddle cinched properly?" Cam bit out. "You should have checked it!"

"I did!" McHugh's face turned as red as his hair. Bending down, he hefted the saddle to his knees. The cinch dragged against the ground. "Somebody must have loosened it. Maybe one of your enemies, Parker," he added with a sneer.

Cam became very quiet and Nancy's interest quickened. Had Cam Parker made the kind of enemies who would stoop to killing his jockey?

McHugh dropped the saddle and vaulted the rail. Cam, as if coming out of a trance, muttered, "I should see to Toot Sweet."

Nancy nodded. Near the other end of the track she could make out Thea and a dozen other track workers finally getting control of the skittish filly. Cam ran in their direction.

"Let's wait at the barns for them," Nancy suggested to Bess, who by now had dusted herself off. "I'd like to ask some questions about that loosened cinch. There's a lot going on here." At Bess's confused look, Nancy explained, "Cam was furious until McHugh zinged him with that line about his enemies."

"What do you think he meant?" Bess wondered.

"I don't know. But—"

"You intend to find out," Bess finished for her. "I know, Nancy. I know."

Nancy smiled to herself. Maybe there actually was a simple explanation for what had happened, but her detective instincts screamed that there was a mystery brewing right there at Churchill Downs. First McHugh's argument with the guy with the broken nose, then the uncinched girth strap, and now the jockey's remark about Cam's enemies.

Bess and Nancy were waiting by Pied Piper's stall when Thea finally returned, looking very worried. Seeing them, she stopped short, surprised. "I'm so sorry. I completely forgot about you two."

"How's Toot Sweet?" Nancy asked.

"Oh, fine. She'd worked herself into a nervous lather, but Cam's got her almost calm now. She's stabled down in barn eight. I don't understand how McHugh could be so careless," she added, sounding angry.

It was clear to Nancy that Cam and Thea laid the blame at the jockey's feet.

Pushing dark strands of hair out of her eyes, Thea said, "Whew! What a day. Why don't you come with me while I check out another Derby favorite, Flash O'Lightnin'. He's working out next. Then we still have time to catch a couple of races before we have to get ready for the party."

"Party?" Bess asked, perking up.

"There's a big party for racehorse owners, trainers, jockeys, and friends tonight," Thea explained. She'd been so involved with Pied Piper and the other horses she'd forgotten to tell the girls about the elegant event.

Bess grabbed Nancy's arm. "Well, let's go see this Flash horse and make tracks out of here, then."

She and Nancy walked with Thea across the stable area to the backstretch rail. There were several clusters of people there already. A gray horse was just charging from the gate. Flash O'Lightnin' looked as fit and hard as Toot Sweet. For a moment, as he tore toward them, Nancy held her breath, afraid that something might happen to Flash and his jockey, too. But the gray horse with the jagged white blaze on its nose galloped around the curve without incident.

"He's going to be tough to beat," Thea predicted. "Even for Toot Sweet."

"Isn't Pied Piper working out today?" Nancy asked. She was anxious to see how her father's Thoroughbred compared to the two favorites.

"His workout was this morning. You'll see him tomorrow," Thea assured her with a smile.

Only fifty feet away Nancy noticed Ken McHugh, his red hair glowing like a beacon, watching Flash through narrowed eyes. Apparently he also thought the colt would be hard to beat.

Beyond Ken stood a beautiful, friendly-looking, dark-haired girl wearing a full-length mink coat. It was late afternoon and still warm. She must be baking, Nancy thought, wondering why she would bother with the elegant fur.

Just after Flash's time was announced over the loudspeaker, Nancy heard the girl's soft laughter. Glancing at her, Nancy noticed that she kept shooting sidelong glances at Ken McHugh.

Nancy had turned to ask Thea who the girl was when Thea muttered under her breath, "Uh-oh. Here comes Eddie Brent. He's Flash's owner and trainer, not to mention the owner of Brentwood Stables in California. The guy with him is Ace Hanford, the jockey who just gave Flash his workout. He's going to ride the colt in the Derby."

"Why did you say 'uh-oh'?" asked Bess.

"You'll see," Thea said grimly.

Eddie Brent and Ace Hanford were walking over to where they were standing by the backstretch rail. "Why didn't you bring out the whip sooner?" Brent demanded of the jockey in a voice loud enough for them all to hear. "Flash was just waiting for you to ask for some speed!"

Ace Hanford stayed calm. He seemed older and more assured than Ken McHugh and Jimmy Harris. Years of working outdoors had etched lines beside his eyes and weathered his skin to a deep bronze. He paid no attention to Eddie Brent's ranting and raving.

"Did you hear Flash's time, Thea, my girl?" Eddie Brent asked when he was at her side. "Flash is looking really fine. I'm afraid that horse of yours doesn't stand a chance." Brent was grinning from ear to ear.

"We're gonna grind Toot Sweet in the finish, you just watch," he continued. "And Pied Piper isn't even in the running."

"Guess we'll just have to prove you wrong, huh?" Thea rejoined, a tight smile barely curving her lips. She pulled Nancy and Bess away as quickly as possible.

"Nice guy," Bess observed sarcastically.

"Eddie talks big," Thea said, "but he's never had a Derby winner. Flash could be the one, though," she added.

They watched the rest of the races, then checked on Pied Piper once again. By the time Nancy and Bess had left the barns to head back to their hotel, dusk had fallen. The track lights began coming on automatically. Soon it would be dark.

"Isn't that Ken McHugh?" Bess asked, pointing ahead of her. McHugh was just exiting the stable area gate, a saddle in his hands.

"It sure is. And look, Bess. There's that girl in the mink coat we saw earlier today."

The girl was inside the stable area, talking to an older man with silvery hair who was wearing a gray flannel suit.

"Who do you suppose she is?" Bess asked, looking at the girl.

"I don't know. Bess, would you mind if I talked to McHugh for just a minute? I'd like to ask him about that girth strap."

"Sure. But make it fast. I don't want to be late to the party, and I still don't know what to do with my hair!" she declared, fidgeting with her baseball cap.

"Mr. McHugh?" Nancy called out as he was heading into the parking lot.

He stopped and turned back, eyeing Nancy warily. "Who wants to know?"

"My name's Nancy Drew. I happened to be

standing by the backstretch rail when your saddle uncinched during the workout earlier. I just wondered—"

"Uncinched?" He laughed harshly.

"Do you have any idea how it happened?" Nancy was about to tell McHugh she was a detective and had overheard the heavyset man threatening him earlier, but it wasn't necessary. McHugh was already holding up the saddle and yanking at the girth strap. He shoved one end of the strap in front of Nancy's nose.

"Does this look *uncinched* to you?" he demanded.

Nancy stared at the strap. The leather had been cut three-quarters of the way through. The rest was torn and frayed where it had broken loose.

"Someone cut this," Nancy said quietly.

McHugh nodded, his nostrils flaring. "You got it right! Someone who wants me dead!"

Chapter

Four

I'VE ALREADY taken this up with the secretary's office!" McHugh said, shaking the strap in his fist and striding swiftly away.

"Do you think someone really meant to kill him?" Bess asked, coming up behind Nancy.

"Well, someone wanted to scare or hurt him pretty badly to cut that strap," Nancy answered thoughtfully. "Or someone wanted to hurt Toot Sweet."

"The horse?" Bess blinked several times. "Do you think it has something to do with that man who was threatening McHugh earlier?"

"Maybe." Nancy slowly shook her head, following McHugh with her eyes. "I wish I knew what that was all about. What did McHugh mean when he told that guy he wasn't 'stiffing'? Remind me to ask Thea."

McHugh passed between several horse trailers. A movement on the other side of a van caught Nancy's eye. "Look, Bess!" she said excitedly, pointing. "Isn't that the man who threatened McHugh?"

Bess squinted against the darkening gloom. "Where?"

"Over there." As Nancy watched, the figure disappeared. "Maybe we should follow McHugh and make sure he's okay."

Bess groaned but agreed. She trailed after Nancy as they picked their way between the vans, trailers, and cars. Suddenly the figure emerged from a shadow and planted itself directly in front of McHugh. It *was* the man who'd threatened McHugh earlier!

"That is the guy!" Nancy whispered excitedly.

At first, the two men argued, but then McHugh waved the heavyset man away and took off in another direction. After a moment the heavyset man went the opposite way.

"Well, I guess that's over for now," Nancy said uneasily. "I wish I'd heard what they were saying, though."

"Come on, Nancy," Bess said. "You've had more than enough mystery for one day." Nancy reluctantly let Bess steer her toward their car. "Besides, we've got a party to get to."

The Carlisle Hotel ballroom was already filled with dozens of elegantly dressed people when Nancy and Bess stepped through the wide double doors.

"Do I look all right?" Bess whispered to Nancy as she paused just inside the room, anxiously fluffing her bangs.

Bess's dress was a strapless powder blue shift with a kick pleat up the back. She had pulled her hair back, twisting it into a sophisticated bun at the nape of her neck.

"You look fabulous," Nancy told her, smoothing down her black strapless gown. The dress sported a cream-colored bolero jacket, and Nancy had looked long and hard for the twisted strands of tiny cream and black jet beads that circled her throat. Her hair hung loose around her shoulders.

"Wow! This is terrific!" Bess cried. "It's so elegant!"

"You're right, Bess," Nancy agreed. "Look, there's Thea."

She and Bess eased their way along the edge of the dance floor toward the trainer. Gone were

29

Thea's work clothes. That night she was wearing a simple white dress that showed off the wonderful tan she'd acquired from spending so much time outdoors. Her dark hair was pulled away from her face with ivory combs and fell in soft curls down her back. Spying Nancy and Bess, she beckoned them to her.

Cam was a few feet away, deep in conversation with Eddie Brent, whose smug grin remained firmly in place even as he talked. From Cam's frosty but polite smile, Nancy suspected Eddie was telling Cam how wonderful Flash O'Lightnin' was.

"Doesn't Cam look great?" Bess whispered in Nancy's ear.

"He sure does," Nancy agreed. In a tuxedo the trainer's good looks were only intensified.

"I was wondering if you two were going to make it," Thea said when Bess and Nancy were in earshot. "I thought for sure you'd beat me here."

"We got delayed," Nancy said, deciding not to explain about McHugh just yet. She wanted to sort through some things in her mind before she told Thea about the cut girth strap.

"Nancy's got another mystery on her brain," Bess explained. "That's why we were delayed. In fact, if it hadn't been for—" Bess stopped short as Nancy gently stepped on her toe.

Thea turned her dark gaze to Nancy. "A mystery?"

"I was just wondering about that man we saw talking to McHugh earlier," Nancy was forced to explain. "Do you know who he might be? He seemed so threatening."

"Well, I doubt if he's an owner, trainer, or jockey," said Thea thoughtfully. "I know most of them."

Nancy glanced over the crowd. She recognized Ace Hanford, Flash O'Lightnin's jockey, standing near the punch bowl. Ken McHugh appeared at that moment and started heading toward Ace.

There was a faint stir in the room, and Nancy followed the crowd's glances toward the door. The girl who'd been wearing the mink coat that afternoon was just entering the ballroom, her hand on the sleeve of the older man she'd been with earlier. She wore a full-length silver lamé gown, and around her neck was the most elaborate diamond necklace Nancy had ever seen. A silver and white fox stole had been artfully thrown over her shoulders to appear casual but elegant. The man with her wore a black formal suit complete with tails. They were a matched pair, like the bride and father of the bride.

"Who on earth is that?" Nancy asked Thea.

Thea's mouth twisted sardonically. "Laura and Evan Johnson."

"Who are they?" Nancy squeezed closer to Thea as the crowd swelled. Bess moved in on Thea's other side.

"Evan Johnson is Laura's father. They're from a well-known Kentucky horse-breeding family. Evan's brother, Ulysses Johnson, was a renowned champion racehorse breeder. He started Johnson Farms and produced more winners for ten years than any other breeder." Thea shook her head in remembered admiration. "U.J., as he called himself, died a few months ago. Since then, Laura and Evan have become a fixture here at Churchill Downs—even though neither one of them knows very much about horses."

"Johnson Farms," Bess repeated. "That's where Toot Sweet's from."

"Uh-huh." Something in Thea's tone made Nancy sense there was more to the story. "Are they running Johnson Farms now?"

"Mmmm," Thea murmured, glancing over at Cam.

Taking that for a yes, Nancy asked, "How does Cam feel about working for them?" She could imagine the kind of problems that might crop up for a trainer when the owners knew next to nothing about horses.

Thea drew a heavy breath. Nancy had the feeling she was weighing her words carefully before she spoke. "Well, it was quite different when Laura's uncle was alive. U.J. was a bit of a tyrant. A lot of people couldn't stand him and there were rumors about some shady business practices. But he knew horses and he trusted Cam."

"So Ken McHugh is one of Johnson Farms' jockeys, then," Bess observed thoughtfully.

Nancy wondered if that was why Laura had been observing McHugh so closely at the racecourse earlier.

"McHugh is distantly related to Laura—I think they're second cousins," explained Thea. She paused a moment, as if uncertain how much to reveal, then shrugged her shoulders. "Anyway, U.J. liked him as a jockey, and he put in his will that McHugh had to be kept on at Johnson Farms."

Nancy glanced over at Cam, who had escaped from Eddie Brent and was now standing with Evan and Laura Johnson. Laura was gazing adoringly into Cam's eyes, but Cam's expression was stony. His eyes were fixed on the girl's father, and it appeared he didn't like what he was hearing.

"If Cam doesn't like working for the Johnsons, why doesn't he leave?" Nancy asked. "Surely there are other horse-breeding farms where—"

"Cam's happy where he is," Thea cut her off unexpectedly. "Does anyone want a glass of punch? I'm dying of thirst." She glanced from

Nancy to Bess, but when both girls shook their heads, she worked her way to the punch bowl alone.

"What was that all about?" Bess wondered aloud.

"I don't know. Thea seemed eager to talk until I mentioned Cam."

"Do you think something serious is going on between Thea and Cam?" Bess asked, glancing wistfully at the handsome, dark-haired trainer.

"Yes, I do," Nancy told her friend, following Bess's gaze. "But it looks like Laura Johnson hasn't figured it out yet."

At that moment Laura detached herself from her father and Cam and wandered in Nancy and Bess's direction. She was sipping from a champagne glass, glancing over the crowd. Nancy put her age at somewhere in her mid-twenties.

"You're Laura Johnson, aren't you?" Nancy asked politely when Laura came within earshot.

"That's right," she said, a friendly smile curving her lips.

"I'm Nancy Drew, and this is my friend Bess Marvin." Realizing she needed some way to connect herself, Nancy added, "I guess you could say I'm a part owner of Pied Piper. My father has a quarter interest in the colt."

"That's interesting," Laura murmured, her eyes scanning the crowd.

"I understand you're Toot Sweet's owner," Nancy pursued.

Laura's lashes swept her cheeks and her lips tightened a fraction. "That's right."

"I saw Toot Sweet work out today," Nancy began, still trying to get the girl's attention.

"That's nice. Look, will you excuse me? There's someone I need to talk to." With that, Laura headed for the crystal champagne fountain.

"For someone so rich, she obviously never was sent to charm school," Bess said, shaking her head. "Should we head over to the punch bowl and get something to drink now?" Bess asked. "I'm thirsty."

"Good idea," Nancy agreed, her gaze landing briefly on Evan Johnson and Ken McHugh, who were directly in her line of vision. Johnson held a champagne glass in his right hand. At that precise moment the glass suddenly shattered into pieces. Nancy gasped. He'd squeezed it so tightly it had broken!

Blood flowed down Evan's hand and onto the ballroom's black-and-white tile floor. A sudden chill made Nancy shiver.

She followed Evan's gaze, which was still fastened on Ken McHugh. There was murder in his eyes!

Chapter

Five

$\mathbf{K}$EN McHUGH casually lifted his glass to his lips. When the jockey lowered the glass, Nancy saw he was smirking as he spun and sauntered toward the door.

Evan Johnson jerked forward, ready to follow the jockey, but Laura quickly moved to his side and stopped him. A waiter handed Evan a towel. Even as he wrapped it around his bleeding hand, he never took his cold gaze from McHugh.

"What just happened?" asked Bess.

"I don't know, but I'm going to find out," Nancy answered as she shifted around several people to join Evan Johnson's group.

As Nancy approached them, Johnson stalked away with Laura trailing after him. Cam and Thea, who were standing nearby, stared after them.

"Do you know what he meant?" Thea was asking Cam as Nancy reached them.

"You know McHugh," Cam said. "He always talks like that."

Nancy and Bess approached the two trainers. "Like what?" Nancy asked pointedly.

Cam's jaw was set, and Nancy didn't think he would answer. Finally he muttered in disgust, "Like he knows secrets about everybody. It's all a big front. He just likes goading people. One day he'll go too far with that big mouth of his!"

"What did McHugh say to upset Evan Johnson so much?" Bess asked curiously.

There was a moment of silence as Thea and Cam glanced at each other. Cam cleared his throat uncomfortably. Nancy could practically feel the tension rising from the two trainers.

Cam sighed and finally spoke up. "McHugh said to Evan, 'Well, you really *fixed* things last March, didn't you?' It's just the kind of crack he's always making, and it infuriated Evan."

"What did he mean by that?" Bess asked blankly.

The wheels were turning in Nancy's mind.

"Was McHugh accusing Evan of fixing a race?" she guessed.

"That's what he made it sound like." Cam shrugged. "But the only way Evan could fix a race was if he bribed a jockey to deliberately hold his horse back during a race."

"Why would he want to do that?" Bess asked, puzzled.

"To eliminate the competition," Nancy explained.

"Don't take anything McHugh says seriously," Cam warned. "He just likes to stir things up."

Nancy was about to ask Cam what he meant when Jimmy Harris, Pied Piper's jockey, looking uncomfortable in his tuxedo, came over and asked Thea to dance with him.

Thea accepted graciously, then someone asked Bess to dance. Left alone with Cam, Nancy was pleased when he suggested they hit the dance floor, too.

"Sure," Nancy said, happy for the chance to follow up on their conversation.

Cam tucked Nancy's hand in his and led her to the center of the floor. He held her lightly in his arms. Nancy had to admit that Bess was right. Cam had a real presence.

"*Could* Evan have fixed a race?" she asked when she felt the moment was right.

Cam smiled faintly. "Thea told me you were a detective. Don't you ever take any time off?"

"Not often," Nancy admitted a bit sheepishly. Cam laughed.

"It would be a pretty tough thing to do," he answered after a moment's thought. "One way would be to have a jockey deliberately hold his horse back. It's called stiffing a horse."

"Stiffing!" Nancy exclaimed, remembering what McHugh had said to the heavyset man with the broken nose.

"That's right. But the catch is, you'd have to have every jockey stiffing except the one riding the horse you bet on. That's a lot of jockeys to buy off if the field's big."

Nancy was thinking fast. The heavyset man had apparently wanted McHugh to stiff Toot Sweet in the Derby, but McHugh refused. She decided to try to talk to McHugh as soon as possible to find out if she was right.

"Is there any other way to fix a race?" she asked Cam.

He nodded. "Horses have been drugged to increase their speed, but now after a race each horse is tested. If there are any drugs present, the horse is disqualified."

Sensing their dance would soon come to an end, Nancy changed the subject to Cam himself.

"How long have you worked for Johnson Farms?"

She felt his muscles tense beneath her hands. "A few years," he answered cautiously.

"Thea said you worked for U.J. first, Evan Johnson's brother," Nancy prodded.

"That's right." He smiled again. "U.J. was one of a kind."

Nancy couldn't tell by his comment whether Cam had liked U.J. or not. "How do you mean?"

"Oh, he loved to rub people the wrong way— kind of like McHugh. They were a lot alike, and I guess that's what U.J. saw in Ken. They were both gamblers, too. Ken's still a pretty heavy bettor at the track."

"I didn't know jockeys could bet on races," remarked Nancy.

"They can bet on their own horse, but the bet has to be placed through the horse's owner or trainer."

"Do you place bets for him?" Nancy asked curiously.

"No way. McHugh and I just barely tolerate each other. I wouldn't go out of my way to do him a favor."

"McHugh and Evan Johnson don't seem to get along too well, either," Nancy observed.

"It goes with the territory, I suppose." Cam

shrugged. "McHugh's too much like U.J. for Evan."

"Evan didn't like his brother?"

Cam laughed. "Evan *hated* his brother. U.J. knew it and loved making things worse." Cam's gaze fell on someone near the door, and Nancy turned to look. "Take Eddie Brent," said Cam. "U.J. hated him, too. Brent's a California breeder and U.J. was a die-hard Kentuckian. They were bitter rivals right to the end."

"It sounds like U.J. didn't have many friends," Nancy murmured. "How did he die?"

"It wasn't foul play, if that's what you think," Cam said quickly. "He'd been sick a long time and died peacefully. I know because I was with him at the end."

The music ended and Cam led Nancy back to where Thea and Bess were waiting. Nancy would have liked to continue their talk, but Cam drew Thea into his arms and onto the dance floor, gazing at her in a way that left no doubt about his feelings.

"So much for wishful thinking." Bess sighed, focusing on Cam.

"I think you're better off without him, anyway," Nancy informed her. "He did tell me a lot about Johnson Farms, but I got the feeling he was holding something back."

41

"I don't really care what he's hiding," Bess declared. "He's absolutely gorgeous."

"On that," Nancy said, catching Cam's handsome profile, "we agree totally!"

The next day Nancy slept late and woke with late-morning sunlight streaming over her face. After tossing back the covers, she dashed to the shower.

"Wake up!" she yelled at Bess, who was sound asleep in the other double bed. "The Derby Trial is today, and Thea told me Ken McHugh's riding another of Johnson Farms' horses."

Bess's only answer was a groan.

By the time Nancy had finished showering and was changing into a pair of khaki shorts and a green polo shirt, Bess was staggering around the room, bleary-eyed.

"What time did we get in last night?" she mumbled, heading for the bathroom.

"Only midnight. But it was a long day."

"Too long," Bess said with a yawn.

Half an hour later Bess stood in front of the dresser mirror, frowning at her reflection. Her lemon yellow sundress looked cool and comfortable. "Do you think my bangs have grown at all?" she asked hopefully.

"Maybe a little," Nancy said.

"Hah. You're just saying that to make me feel better." Bess snatched up a floppy straw hat with a yellow flowered band and plopped it on her head. "I love hats," she declared happily.

They arrived at the racecourse to find the parking lot even more crowded than the day before. The noise from the grandstands was deafening. Each day closer to the Derby meant bigger crowds, Nancy realized.

"What's the Derby Trial?" Bess asked, peering over Nancy's shoulder at a brochure.

"The main race of the day. It's the last one, at five-thirty, so we've got most of the afternoon to kill. Let's find Pied Piper."

Bess and Nancy stayed near the barns during most of the afternoon. By the time of the Derby Trial, Nancy had checked out Pied Piper and the other thirteen horses who would be racing in the Trial. They all were strong and powerful.

"One of the Thoroughbreds, Midnight Express, is also from Johnson Farms," Nancy said out loud, reading from her program. She and Bess had gone down to the track and were crowded against the infield rail at the far turn. "He's the only one in this race who's slotted for the Derby."

"There are Cam and Thea!" Bess cried, waving across the track at the couple. They waved back.

"I can't see the starting gate from here," Bess complained, standing on tiptoe to peer over the sea of heads.

"We'll see them when they get to the home-stretch," Nancy reassured her. "Besides, we can see the finish line from here, and that's better than the starting gate."

Suddenly they heard the clang of the gates. A roar went up from the crowd and almost drowned out the thundering hoofbeats.

Nancy strained to see. Johnson Farms' colors were black and red. Would Ken McHugh's black-and-red silks be in the lead?

"I can't see!" Bess complained again.

"Just wait. They're coming!"

Horses pounded around the curve, leaning in, four or five bunched together. Nancy craned her neck to see Ken McHugh. Where was he?

Her gaze fell on the sixth horse. Hugging the rail, Midnight Express was straining hard but losing ground. Then she saw McHugh in the lead. Instead of crouching gracefully over the horse, he was weaving on top of the charging colt as if he could barely hold on!

Gasping, Nancy watched as he swayed far to the left. The jockey's head bounced against the infield rail, and his helmet unsnapped and fell off.

McHugh then plunged from the colt in a tumble of black and red, smashing full force against the rail and landing facedown in the dirt track. The pounding field of horses was thundering straight toward his still form!

Chapter

Six

WATCH OUT!" Nancy cried, her voice lost in the screams of the crowd. The nearest horses leapt over McHugh's body, saving him from their pounding hooves.

Nancy struggled to get through the crush of people and over the rails to McHugh, but the track marshals and medics got to the jockey first.

"Get back, everyone!" one of them ordered. "Get back!"

The wail of a track ambulance siren sounded. Nancy, Cam, and Thea watched as a medic gave Ken McHugh artificial respiration. Another medic then clamped an oxygen mask over his face, and the two men lifted him into the back of the waiting ambulance.

Quietly, the others headed back toward the barns. Thea was pressed close to Cam's side, his arm around her. Nancy and Bess walked a few paces ahead, giving them some privacy. Still, Nancy could hear the conversation between the two trainers.

In a low, shaky voice, Thea said to Cam, "If Ken dies, the rumors will start again. I just know they will."

"Shhh," Cam warned.

"We've got to do something, Cam," Thea whispered. "Before it's too late!"

"Don't worry. I'll handle it," Cam reassured her softly.

Nancy desperately wanted to know what Cam could handle, but right then didn't seem like the time to ask.

By unspoken consent, they all stopped at Toot Sweet's stall. Cam was checking the filly, when Nancy heard sharp, rapid footsteps behind them.

She turned to see Laura Johnson, in a stunning white silk dress and jacket, hurrying toward them. Her face was nearly as white as the fabric.

"Oh, Cam," she cried. "Isn't it awful? I'm so afraid!" She threw herself into his arms. Cam looked surprised, but he didn't push her away.

Thea sucked in a breath. Swallowing, she turned on her heel and strode away.

"Thea! Wait!" Cam called, but Thea kept on going. He started to follow after her, but Laura hung on to his arm.

"Ken's not going to die, is he?" she asked in a shaky voice.

Nancy and Bess left Cam with Laura and followed Thea back to Pied Piper's stall. The girls found her inside the colt's stall, brushing him down, her face set.

"I need a little time alone," she told them, without looking up from the colt's glossy coat.

"Sure," Nancy said, seeing there was nothing to do to console the girl. She nodded at Bess. "I think we'll go back to the hotel. Let us know if you hear anything about Ken McHugh."

Nancy and Bess had been back at the hotel about two hours when Thea called with the news. "He's in a coma," she said quietly. "They don't know if he's going to make it."

Nancy's stomach turned. "Thanks for letting us know," she answered softly before hanging up.

The look on Nancy's face was enough explanation for Bess. "Oh, no," Bess murmured.

The phone rang again. This time it was Nancy's father. "How's everything going?" Carson asked.

"Not so great, Dad," Nancy admitted, telling him about the jockey's fall.

Carson listened quietly. "What a terrible accident," he said finally, "but it happens in racing sometimes."

"I know," Nancy murmured. "But it worries me that McHugh said he thought someone wanted him dead." Remembering the cut girth strap, she added, "Maybe his accident wasn't really an accident."

"I'm sure the track officials are looking into it," her father assured her.

"I hope you're right," Nancy said grimly. After talking for a few more minutes, she hung up. Bess convinced her to go down to the hotel coffee shop to have a bite to eat, and afterward the two girls went back to the room. While Bess watched TV, Nancy lay on her bed and stared up at the ceiling, reflecting on her father's words. "It happens in racing. . . ."

But does it? Nancy asked herself. Someone had obviously cut McHugh's girth. Did that same person somehow cause this accident? Why hadn't she checked out the horse and saddle? Nancy chided herself. Now she'd have to get her information secondhand.

Wednesday morning Nancy had promised Bess they would sightsee and shop in Louisville for a couple of hours. They spent the time strolling down the town's main streets, but Nancy couldn't think of anything but getting back to the track.

Over a snack at an outdoor café, Nancy finally burst out, "Bess, do you mind if we go out to the track? I can't stand not knowing what's going on."

"No problem," said Bess. "I have to admit, I don't really feel like shopping today."

"That's a first," Nancy teased, but she understood. McHugh's accident had put a damper on their spirits.

When they arrived at the racecourse everything looked like business as usual. Several horses were working out on the track with the ever-present race reporters, stopwatches in hand, lining the rail.

"Too bad about McHugh," Nancy heard one of the reporters mutter as she and Bess walked by.

"Yeah," his companion answered. "Could cost the filly the race."

Eddie Brent stood near the stable area fence next to a heavy man. Nancy did a double take, but a second look told her Eddie's companion wasn't the man she'd seen talking to McHugh that first day. This guy was writing down notes. Another reporter, Nancy realized.

"McHugh was just reckless," Eddie was saying in an offhand manner. "His heart was never really in racing. He liked the money. Period. Ask anybody. But he always put a little too much of it down on the horses, you know what I mean?" he asked slyly.

Nancy wrinkled her nose in distaste. Eddie Brent might own one of the classiest breeding farms in California, but he had no class. He was sensationalizing McHugh's accident!

Cam, Thea, and Laura Johnson were standing outside Toot Sweet's box. Following the direction of Laura's gaze, Nancy knew that Cam was her primary interest, not Toot Sweet.

"Hi." Thea greeted Nancy and Bess with a relieved smile. She seemed glad that someone had come to break up their little threesome.

"Hi," Nancy and Bess chorused.

"Any news on Ken McHugh's condition?" Nancy asked the group at large.

"He's still in a coma," Cam answered soberly. "We're going to have to get another jockey for the Derby."

Nancy glanced at Laura, who was smoothing a single strand of her beautifully styled dark hair back in place. The girl was wearing a set of teardrop diamond earrings and a pink-and-green floral print dress. A single strand of diamonds

51

adorned her left wrist. "Well, don't look at me," she said with a laugh. "Ask Cam who he's asking to ride."

Nancy glanced expectantly at the trainer, but Bess continued staring at Laura. Cam answered her unasked question. "I asked Walt Collins, who also rides for us pretty steadily, to be Toot Sweet's jockey. He's arriving tonight."

Laura closed her eyes and shuddered delicately, as if she'd just been reminded of an unpleasant topic. "Did you hear there might be an investigation into Ken's accident?" she asked in a hushed voice.

Thea's breath caught. "Really?" Nancy murmured.

"Well, it's a waste of time," Cam snapped.

"I agree with Cam," Thea said, surprising Nancy. "It's all just rumors anyway."

"Rumors?" Nancy asked, exchanging a look with a surprised Bess. "What kind of rumors?"

"There haven't been any rumors about McHugh," Cam clarified, shooting a warning at Thea to be quiet. Nancy not the look.

"Well, I'm going back to the hotel to change for dinner," Laura announced, ending the conversation. "You're coming with Daddy and me tonight, aren't you?" she asked Cam in a pleading voice.

"I'll be there after I pick Walt up," Cam said with a sigh.

Laura left when a stable boy called Cam to check out one of the other Johnson Farms horses.

"Let's go to the races," Thea suggested, her voice a little tight. Nancy wondered if she was upset with Cam for trying to keep her quiet, or with Laura for flirting so openly with her boyfriend.

The Wednesday afternoon races were on when Nancy, Bess, and Thea found places to stand at the rail. The reporter who'd been interviewing Eddie Brent was now talking rapidly to several people Nancy recognized as track personnel.

"I'm telling you, it's a fact," the reporter declared loudly. "McHugh's bloodstream was loaded with sedatives. He didn't have an accident. Someone tried to kill him!"

Chapter

Seven

"KILL HIM!" Thea cried out.

The reporter glanced back at Bess, Nancy, and Thea. Apparently he didn't think they were important, so he turned back to the others he'd been talking to.

Thea was white as a sheet. "Attempted murder," she muttered in a trembling voice. "No, it can't be."

"If he'd been given a sedative, that would explain why he slid off the horse," said Nancy. "He was passing out and couldn't hold on."

Thea pressed her fingers to her lips, her eyes huge. "He would have known in the starting gate that something was wrong. Why would he take such a risk?"

"Maybe he didn't understand what was happening," Bess suggested.

"But who would have done such a thing?" Thea asked, her face pale.

Nancy remembered Cam's comment about McHugh's big mouth getting him into trouble someday. Did Cam have a reason for wanting McHugh dead or know of someone who wanted him dead?

"I know you won't believe all the rumors, just the facts," Thea suddenly put in.

Nancy was about to ask Thea what she meant, but she was interrupted by a police officer. Like the reporter, the police officer had been interviewing racing officials and personnel. According to the officer, the police had been called in to investigate both of McHugh's accidents. McHugh had shown the cut girth strap to someone in the secretary's office, and that initial incident had been reported to the police.

"We're putting Mr. McHugh under police protection," the officer added after he had finished his questions. "In case we uncover foul play."

After he left, Nancy turned thoughtfully to Bess. "I think I'll do a little investigating on my own. I'd like to locate our mystery man with the smashed nose and find out exactly what he was trying to get Ken McHugh to do."

Saying a quick goodbye to Thea, Nancy and Bess took off for the stables. They spent the afternoon asking the stable boys, grooms, jockeys, trainers, and owners if anyone had ever seen the heavyset man who'd threatened McHugh. No one volunteered any information, but Nancy got the distinct impression that some of the stable boys and jockeys knew who she was asking about. They just wouldn't talk.

"It's so frustrating," Nancy complained to Bess late that afternoon when they hadn't come up with a single lead. "Why won't anyone talk about this guy?"

"He must be really bad news," Bess offered, resting her hands on her hips. That day Bess had dressed in denim shorts and an aqua tank top. Her hair was clipped away from her face, and she seemed to have forgotten the trauma of her bangs.

"You were really staring at Laura earlier," Nancy remembered. "What were you thinking about?"

"Nothing much. But you know that dress she was wearing? I saw it a few years ago. It was by a really trendy European designer."

"A few years ago?" Nancy's brows lifted. "Laura doesn't seem the type to wear anything that isn't this year's style."

"That's what I thought. She's too concerned about her appearance to be caught dead in something that old."

They were strolling in front of the barns when they saw Cam coming through the stable gate. Beside him was a short blond man who Nancy guessed was Toot Sweet's new jockey.

Bess stopped short as Cam and the shorter man headed their way. Walt Collins, Nancy remembered, as Cam began to introduce him.

"Walt's one of the best jockeys around," Cam finished as the jockey shook hands with Nancy, then Bess. His hair was a thatch of unruly gold that fell appealingly over his forehead. His eyes were a brilliant sky blue.

"Nice to meet you, Walt," Nancy said, amused at the way Walt's gaze was centered on Bess. Bess, Nancy realized in amusement, was staring back at him.

"Nice to meet you, too," Walt answered, still looking at Bess.

With Bess and Walt standing so close together, Nancy was struck by how much they looked alike—both blond and cute! Bess had that starry-eyed look Nancy knew so well. She had already fallen for Walt!

"I hate to break this up," Cam said dryly, "but we've got work to do."

"Are you going to be around later?" Walt asked Bess pointedly.

She nodded vigorously. "Nancy's father is part owner of Pied Piper. We're here with the colt."

"Great. I'll catch you later!" he said, taking off at a jog to catch up with Cam, who had gone on ahead.

"Isn't he the cutest?" Bess said breathily.

"I thought you had a crush on Cam," Nancy answered innocently.

"Who, me? Oh, no. Cam's great looking and all, but he's only interested in Thea. Besides"— Bess's dimple showed—"you know I'm a sucker for blonds."

"Five-foot-tall blonds?" Nancy asked.

"Oh, I know he's kind of short. A couple inches shorter than me, actually," Bess admitted. "But who cares?" She looked stricken. "You don't suppose he could weigh less than I do, do you?"

Nancy grinned. "A Derby horse can only carry one hundred and twenty-six pounds with the saddle."

Bess groaned. "That does it. I'm going to have to skip dinner tonight. Remind me, will you? Well, at least I won't eat anything fattening."

Nancy laughed, then noticed Eddie Brent outside one of the last barns in the row. "There's Eddie Brent. I'd like to find out what he thinks about McHugh's accident."

Brent was berating a stable boy for apparently not looking after Flash as he should have. The stable boy was saying nothing, but his anger showed in his tightly clenched jaw.

"Good luck," Bess said with feeling, falling into step beside Nancy.

"Hello, Mr. Brent." Nancy introduced herself with a smile. "We haven't officially met, but I'm Nancy Drew. My father's part owner of Pied Piper, and I'm here as the representative owner."

"Oh?" He shook Nancy's outstretched hand, assessing her carefully.

In her peripheral vision Nancy saw Ace Hanford, Flash's jockey, lean against the edge of Flash's stall, unabashedly eavesdropping on their conversation. Good, Nancy thought. If Eddie couldn't help her, maybe Ace could.

"I'm a detective," she told Eddie, "and I'm looking into the circumstances surrounding Ken McHugh's accident. I heard you talking to a reporter earlier. Would you mind—"

"Forget it," Eddie declared, his scowl deepening. "Detective?" He looked at her as if he found it hard to believe. "I don't talk to detectives. Why don't you mind your own business?"

"You wouldn't happen to know a heavyset

man who looks as if his nose has been broken?" Nancy called after him as he stalked away. "I'd really like to speak to him. He was talking to McHugh here at the track on Monday."

Eddie disappeared down the row of stalls, pointedly ignoring her. Nancy sighed. She'd struck out again.

"Nice guy," Bess muttered sardonically.

Nancy's eyes met Ace's. He was still leaning against the stall. Glancing in both directions, he said just loud enough for her to hear, "Come back here tonight, around nine, alone." Then he quickly walked away.

"Now, what do you suppose that was all about?" Bess asked, amazed.

Nancy's eyes sparkled. "I don't know, but it looks as though I'm about to get my first solid lead!"

It was dark and a brisk wind had kicked up by the time Nancy and Bess returned to Churchill Downs that night. They'd changed from shorts to jeans and each had thrown on a lightweight jacket. Wanting to blend into the predominantly male scene, Nancy had tucked her hair into a cap. Now she could almost pass for one of the stable boys.

"Are you sure you don't want me to go over to

meet Ace with you?" Bess asked for the third time.

"He said for me to come alone," Nancy reminded her friend.

"I know, but that's spooky. These barns are dark at night. There aren't a lot of lights on."

"Don't worry, Bess. The stable boys sleep on cots in the barns to guard the horses." Nancy smiled assuredly. "I'll be fine."

They ran into Walt outside of Toot Sweet's barn, and as soon as he spied Bess, he came running over. "You want to go down to the stable cafeteria? I bring my own food, but we could get tea or something."

"You bring your own food?" Bess repeated curiously.

Walt nodded. "Strictly healthy stuff. I can't eat all the grease and preservatives they pack into cafeteria food."

Knowing Bess's love for french fries and chocolate, Nancy wondered how her infatuation with Walt was going to turn out. "I'll meet you both at the cafeteria later," she said, chuckling to herself as she headed for the barn where Flash O'Lightnin' was stabled.

Although the racecourse had outdoor lights, there were many dark shadows, and as Nancy approached Flash's barn, she noticed there wasn't a single light on. Thea had told her earlier that the gray colt had been stabled away from most of the other entries because he was extremely nervous and excitable.

Wishing she'd brought her penlight, Nancy shoved her hands in the pockets of her jacket and strode toward Flash's stall.

Peering into the gloomy barn, Nancy was struck by how eerily quiet it was. Where were the grooms and stable boys who slept in the barns to watch over the Derby horses? she wondered uneasily, not daring to go inside. Why wasn't anyone watching over Flash?

Hearing a noise at the far end of the barn, Nancy turned sharply. A shadowy figure was just disappearing around the far corner. Was it Ace? If so, why was he being so secretive?

Nancy followed the intruder. On the ground just in front of her lay a riding crop. Picking it up, she wondered if it was Ace's.

"Mr. Hanford?" she called softly.

There was no answer except for the moaning sound of the wind. Nancy headed back to the barn entrance and crossed inside. Surely Ace wouldn't allow the colt to be completely alone.

She could hear Flash's shuffling hooves long before she saw him. Alert to her presence, the colt suddenly snorted and restlessly pawed the straw.

Nancy opened her mouth to say something soothing to him when a strong arm shot in front of her, pinning her arms to her sides. Before she could scream a hand was clapped across her mouth.

"Move it!" a voice growled.

Nancy's blood ran cold. She struggled to get free, but the hands held her tight. She was being dragged toward the dark, empty end of the barn!

Chapter

Eight

"WHO ARE YOU and what do you want?" a
familiar voice demanded in Nancy's ear.

She stopped struggling instantly. It was Ace!

"Don't yell, or you'll scare the horse," he
ordered, releasing his hand from her mouth.

"Mr. Hanford, it's me," Nancy managed to say
after taking a deep breath.

The jockey muttered an oath and twisted her
around, staring through the gloom at her face.
"Nancy Drew? I didn't recognize you in that hat
and jacket! What were you doing sneaking up on
Flash with that crop? You could have scared him
into hurting himself!"

He escorted her outside the barn and into the cool dark night. A small sliver of a moon turned Ace's face a ghostly gray.

"I'm sorry," Nancy apologized. "Where are the stable boys? Who's watching Flash?"

"I am. Flash is real skittish, and I stay at the barn with him most of the time." He glanced over his shoulder toward Flash's stall. "I gave the stable boys the night off. I wanted to talk to you alone."

"But you weren't guarding the horse when I got here," Nancy pointed out.

"I heard something," Ace admitted. "Like somebody walking real soft. So I went to see who it was. When I got back, you were heading for Flash with this in your hand!" He lifted the crop. "Why did you bring it with you, anyway?"

"I found it beside the barn," Nancy told him. "Someone must have dropped it."

Ace grunted. "Probably that stable boy Eddie was so mad at. He used it on Flash earlier, and the horse nearly hurt himself."

"Did you find whoever was walking around the barn?" Nancy asked.

"No," the jockey growled, glancing toward Flash's stall once more. Nancy heard the colt shuffling in the hay. "Look, I don't have a lot of time," Ace went on, his voice low and secretive, "but I heard you asking about Dollar Bill, and I thought maybe it was time I said my piece about the crook."

"Dollar Bill?" Nancy questioned.

"The man you were looking for. The one you saw talking to McHugh. That's Dollar Bill."

"Just who is Dollar Bill?" asked Nancy, keeping her own voice just as quiet.

Ace's expression darkened. "He's a bookie and a crook. You can place any kind of bet with Dollar Bill, but you'd better pay up quick."

Nancy frowned. "He was threatening McHugh when I saw him, telling him he'd better get the money or else."

"That's Bill," Ace said, nodding. "He's got half the jockeys around here scared to death. If you don't pay, he puts the squeeze on you in other ways, you know what I mean? I know he was leaning on McHugh. Wanted him to stiff a horse in the Derby. McHugh said no way."

"Dollar Bill is into race fixing?" Nancy's heart was pounding now. She finally had a solid lead!

Ace nodded grimly. "Among other things. The man's like a bad wind blowing across horse racing."

Nancy's mind was clicking as she sorted through the facts. "So McHugh placed bets with Dollar Bill, then couldn't pay up when he lost," she concluded. "What I don't get is why McHugh went through Bill when he could place a legitimate bet at the track?"

Ace shook his head emphatically. "No, ma'am. Jockeys can only bet on the mount they're riding, and then they can only place the bet—"

"Through the horse's trainer or owner. That's right," Nancy finished, remembering what Cam had told her. She also recalled that McHugh was a heavy gambler. "So McHugh placed some illegal bets, lost, and couldn't come up with the money?"

Ace nodded. "That's right. McHugh had talked Bill into waiting until the Derby. He was going to bet on Toot Sweet and get his money back. But then he fell," Ace said, shaking his head sadly.

"Do you think Bill could have drugged Ken McHugh?" Nancy asked.

"It's possible, but not likely. I mean, Bill wants his money. Until McHugh's better, he won't get it."

Nancy couldn't argue with Ace's logic. Dollar Bill had to want McHugh unharmed—at least until he was paid off.

Glancing once more toward the barn, Ace said, "I've got to get back to Flash, but don't tell anyone I was the one who told you about Dollar Bill, see?"

Nancy saw. From what Ace had said, Dollar Bill was one tough and powerful crook. If he knew Ace was the person who'd fingered him, he might do more than just threaten the jockey. "I won't tell," she assured him.

Ace nodded and disappeared back toward the barns. Nancy stood for a moment in silence, listening. A light snapped on, and for a moment she saw Ace checking out Flash O'Lightnin'. He glanced her way but made no gesture of acknowledgment. From now on, it looked as though Ace Hanford was going to pretend he had no idea who she was.

Nancy was lost in thought when she found Bess and Walt at the cafeteria. She was surprised to see how crowded it was at nine-thirty at night but decided everyone treated it like a social club. She waved to them as she ordered some french fries at the counter, then joined them at the table. Bess looked at her questioningly, but Nancy didn't want to reveal what Ace had said in front of Walt.

Suddenly Nancy saw Cam burst through the cafeteria doors. His face was filled with suppressed anger. Spying Walt, he walked toward their table.

"We've got problems," Cam said to Walt, ignoring Nancy and Bess. "Someone's been snooping around the stables tonight. The stable boys say the horses have been restless. Thea and I are both sleeping on cots in the barns—I don't know what's going on, but I don't like it."

"I'll be on the lookout," Walt said, worried.

"Did you say someone's snooping around?" Nancy asked, thinking of the mysterious figure both she and Ace had seen around Flash's stall. She wished she could talk to Cam alone, but it was clear to her that right then wasn't the proper time.

"Yep. I don't like prowlers. Someone might be trying to harm the horses." Cam's steely blue eyes focused on a table across the room. "So that same someone could win!"

Cam's gaze was directed straight at Eddie Brent, leaving no doubt about who he meant. Before anyone could say anything, Cam was on his way to Eddie's table.

"I wouldn't put it past an owner as shady as Eddie Brent to dope horses or jockeys just so Flash can win the Derby!" he shouted as he went.

The room grew silent. Eddie Brent's face twisted in hatred.

Slowly the owner rose from his chair. The two men squared off as the last few voices hushed. Then— in a lightning move—Brent smashed his fist right into Cam's face!

Chapter

Nine

CUPS AND SAUCERS shattered on the floor as Cam went flying across one of the cafeteria tables. Bess jumped out of her chair. Nancy rushed to help Cam as another man grabbed Brent's arm, holding him back.

Cam got to his feet, holding the left side of his jaw, his eyes cold with rage.

Brent glared right back. "Better watch your mouth, Parker," he growled furiously, "or I might send the police sniffing around your door!"

"Someone's been bothering the horses at night," Cam said tightly. "That someone is you, Brent!"

Eddie sneered, "Try getting your facts straight before you start making accusations!" A smile curved the corners of his mouth, but there was no warmth in it. "While we're pointing fingers, McHugh's accident sure makes it seem like history repeating itself, eh?"

"Cam," Nancy murmured, placing a hand on his arm, "let's get out of here."

The trainer's face was tense, and for just a second, fear flared in his blue eyes. Brent touched a sore spot, Nancy thought. But what did his comment mean?

Cam turned without another word, stalking across the room. As he was leaving, he turned once more to Brent. "Just stay away from the horses," he warned, then pushed through the doors.

Nancy, with Walt and Bess right behind her, followed Cam outside.

"I'd better go with him," Walt said. The jockey strode after Cam, the wind ruffling his blond hair as he disappeared into the night.

"What was that all about?" Bess asked.

"Someone's been hanging around the barns," said Nancy. "Come on, I'll tell you everything I know on the way back to the hotel. Wait till you hear what Ace told me about Dollar Bill!" she added excitedly.

"Dollar Bill?"

"It's a long story," Nancy said, guiding Bess toward the car. On the ride back, she quickly brought her friend up to date on what she had found out. By the time she finished they were back in their hotel room, getting ready for bed.

"So you're going to try to find this bookie?" Bess asked, drawing the sheet up to her chin.

Nancy yawned and stretched. "First thing tomorrow morning," she agreed. "And I have a strong feeling that when we find Dollar Bill, we'll be closer than ever to finding out exactly what's going on."

"I'm sorry I made us late," Bess apologized the next morning as she and Nancy hurried through the wire gate and across the stable area toward the track. The two friends were dressed alike in jeans, tank tops, and oversize cotton shirts.

"That's all right," Nancy said. "It didn't take you as long as usual to get ready."

Bess grabbed Nancy's arm and pointed toward the track. "Look! There's Pied Piper!"

Churning up the dirt, the chestnut colt was flying around the backstretch turn. The crowd standing around the rails watching was even bigger than the day before.

Stopwatches clicked as Pied Piper flashed by the last furlong pole, going at a fast working clip with Jimmy Harris high in the stirrups. Thea had her hair plaited in a single black braid that was in stark contrast to her white windbreaker. She was standing against the rail.

"Fast," a race reporter remarked, glancing at the time.

"Very fast," another one echoed.

Thea glanced up to see Nancy and Bess, a smile on her face. "Pied Piper's fit and ready," she said for the reporters' benefit. "He's in great shape." She shoved her hands into her pockets for protection against the brisk morning.

"What happened to the balmy Kentucky weather?" Bess complained, rubbing her arms with her hands.

"It'll warm up soon," said Thea, glancing at the sun. "If the weather stays like this, the track will be lightning fast for the Derby."

"Have you got a few minutes to talk?" Nancy asked. She wanted to ask the trainer about Dollar Bill and try to find out what Brent's comment about history repeating itself meant the night before. Chances were that Thea would be more approachable than Cam.

Thea's dark eyes assessed Nancy. "Sure. Jimmy's going to cool down Pied Piper and take him back to the stall, so I've got a few minutes."

Glancing over at the empty grandstands, Nancy said, "Why don't we sit down there?"

"Sure." Thea shrugged.

Nancy, Bess, and Thea walked in silence. Thea's brows were drawn together. "What did you want to know?" she asked, nervously perching on the edge of a bench.

First Nancy brought up what she knew about Dollar Bill, carefully omitting her source. Thea looked at her wide-eyed.

"You didn't know about him?" Nancy asked.

She shook her head. "Sure, there're bookies who place illegal bets, but I don't know about this guy specifically. You think he's involved in McHugh's accident?" she asked in an eager rush.

"Maybe." Nancy eyed her thoughtfully. "It sounds like you want him to be."

Thea instantly pulled herself in, her shoulders hunched. She shivered. "I just want the police to find whoever drugged McHugh and get it over with."

"Thea," Nancy said gently, "I think you're protecting Cam."

Thea visibly jumped. "What do you mean?"

Nancy took a deep breath and started in.

"More than once I've heard you say you're worried about rumors. And then I overheard Eddie Brent make a remark to Cam about McHugh's accident being like history repeating itself."

"Eddie said that?" Thea gasped.

"Yes, he did. What do you think he meant?"

When Thea didn't respond immediately, Nancy added gently, "Ken McHugh was drugged. The police are hard at work trying to find who did it. Whatever rumors you're trying to hide are bound to crop up when they start asking questions."

"It's all so unfair!" Thea burst out bitterly, her face twisting with anguish. "Cam and I want to get married, but Cam won't set a date until the rumors have died off completely."

Bess's face drew up in a worried frown. It was clear her heart went out to the girl.

"What rumors?" Nancy asked gently.

Thea sighed. "I guess I might as well tell you. Cam used to work for another horse-breeding farm. He had an excellent reputation and trained a lot of winners, but the premier jockey who rode for them couldn't stand him. There were constant fights. One day Cam caught the jockey stealing some money from his wallet."

"What happened?" Nancy asked expectantly.

"Cam went to the owner, and the jockey was fired. Then the jockey spread all kinds of rumors about Cam—all of them completely untrue!"

"What kind of rumors?" Bess asked.

"Oh, that he was placing illegal bets, fixing races—terrible things! And then—" Thea cut herself off as if she couldn't go on.

"And then?" Nancy prodded.

"And then the jockey died in a stable accident," the trainer said flatly. "It was proved to be just an accident, but suddenly everyone believed all the rumors he'd spread before he died! Cam was even accused of being responsible for the jockey's death." Thea snorted. "It was ridiculous, of course, but he lost his job. And then no one would hire him. He couldn't get work."

Nancy looked down at the track, watching a Derby hopeful work out. "Enter U.J.," she murmured, understanding for the first time why Cam had worked for the irascible owner.

Thea glanced at Nancy, and she looked surprised at the girl's perception. "That's right. U.J. offered Cam the position of head trainer for Johnson Farms. It was a great opportunity. Cam jumped at the chance. U.J., for all his faults, understood horses and racing and everything that went with it. He *knew* how good Cam was." She smiled crookedly. "He didn't pay him very well, but U.J. was notoriously tight. Cam got his chance to work with top-class Thoroughbreds again, and things were looking up."

"Then U.J. died," Nancy said, picking up the thread of the story, "and people suspected Cam of being responsible."

Thea nodded. "That's right. U.J. had been sick a long time. Everyone knew it. But Cam got blamed for his death, anyway!" She pounded her right fist against her knee. "People were jealous of Cam's success and just wanted to believe awful things about him."

Now Nancy understood what Ken McHugh had meant about Cam having enemies. There were people who simply didn't trust him, or envied him.

"Then when Cam inherited the farm, that was just the icing on the cake," Thea finished bitterly.

Nancy blinked and looked at Bess. Her friend simply shrugged her shoulders, obviously as confused as she was.

"*Cam* inherited the farm?" Nancy repeated in disbelief. "What about Evan and Laura?"

Thea looked down at her clenched hands. "As I understand it, Evan was cut out of everything, even the house. Laura was left that. Evan and U.J. didn't get along. In fact, Evan's been away from Kentucky most of his life. He just returned since U.J. died." She shook her head. "I don't think Evan and Laura even saw each other that much until he learned what she'd inherited. Laura owns the breeding rights," she explained.

"You mean other owners pay Laura for the right to breed their horses with hers?" Bess asked.

Thea nodded.

"But Cam owns the farm and animals," Bess repeated.

"That's right," Thea answered defensively, obviously resenting the implication. "If you're thinking Cam had a motive to kill U.J., forget it. Cam may own the farm, but Laura's got the breeding rights, and Ken McHugh inherited seventy-five percent of all the winnings from any Johnson Farms Thoroughbred. The amount of money Cam earns from racing barely keeps the farm going. McHugh was the one with all the money!"

Nancy stared at her. "Ken McHugh inherited seventy-five percent of all Johnson Farms' winnings? Cam only gets twenty-five percent?"

Thea nodded. "That's right."

An awful thought went through Nancy's mind. And who gets that seventy-five percent if Ken McHugh dies? she wondered. Cameron Parker?

"I don't understand," Bess said later that afternoon as she and Nancy relaxed by the hotel pool. As Thea had predicted, the weather had turned warm and balmy. "How could McHugh be desperate for money when he was earning seventy-five percent of the winnings? Isn't that a lot? There are tons of horse races, and Johnson Farms raises a lot of winners."

"McHugh is a heavy gambler," Nancy reminded her. "He could have lost a lot of money. It might take a lot of winners to recoup his losses."

"What a waste," Bess said with a sigh. "I just hope the police catch Dollar Bill."

Nancy felt the sun hot on her face as she closed her eyes and leaned back against her lounge chair. Dollar Bill, she thought. Ken McHugh's accident could have been caused by the crooked bookie, but it didn't seem likely.

Thinking of what Thea had told her, Nancy leapt to her feet and pulled a knee-length T-shirt over her bikini. "I'll be right back," she told Bess. "I've got to talk to my dad."

She hurried back to her room and placed a call to her father's office. Luckily, she caught him in.

"I need you to do me a favor," she said after bringing him up-to-date on Pied Piper and Ken McHugh's accident. "Is there any way you can find out the contents of Ulysses Johnson's will? I know some of what it contains, but I'd like to have the details."

"I'll do what I can," Carson promised.

"And, Dad, could you find out if Ken McHugh has a will? I want to know who his heirs are."

"I might have to pull a few strings to find out," her father answered, a smile in his voice. "How is McHugh, by the way? Any change?"

"No. He's still in a coma, the last I heard," Nancy answered soberly. "Dad, I've been doing some hard thinking about who would want to hurt McHugh," she added.

"Any conclusions?"

"One." She drew in a long breath, afraid to even voice the thought.

"If Ken McHugh dies," she said finally, "it's possible that his seventy-five percent of the winnings reverts to the farm."

"And?" her father prodded. "What are you thinking, Nancy?"

"Then Cam inherits it all. I hate to say it, Dad, but that gives him a prime motive for murder!"

Chapter

Ten

"How do I look?" Bess asked, striking a pose in front of Nancy. In peach cotton pants, a matching oversize shirt, and a silver belt cinching the shirt in, Bess was the picture of chic.

"Terrific," Nancy proclaimed.

"Thanks." Bess fluffed her bangs in the mirror. "What are you going to do tonight while I go out with Walt?"

"Actually," Nancy said, smiling thoughtfully, "I'm going back to the track."

"So late?" Bess asked.

Nancy nodded. "I think I'll ask Thea if I can sleep on a cot in the barn tonight. I want to be

81

there if the person who's been snooping around shows up again."

Bess hesitated. "Do you want me to stay at the barn with you?" she asked bravely.

"Thanks, but no. You could do me a favor, though. When you're out with Walt tonight, see what you can find out about Johnson Farms."

"Sure. Anything else?"

Nancy frowned. "Nope. Except have a good time."

"I'll try my best," Bess said, dimpling.

After Walt picked Bess up, Nancy's mind turned back to the mystery. Cam had mentioned that Walt was a great jockey. Why, then, had Ken McHugh been chosen to ride Toot Sweet in the Derby? Unless her theories were right and McHugh's earnings for Johnson Farms would revert to Cam. If that was the case, Cam might be very interested in having McHugh ride—just to make sure he had a fatal accident.

Nancy mulled over the facts as she drove to the track. Cam seemed honest enough, but she'd seen ample evidence of his hot temper. Had he let his emotions run away with him this time?

When Nancy had asked Thea if she could sleep at the barn, Thea promised to give her an extra cot and sleeping bag. All Nancy brought with her was her purse and her penlight. She wasn't going to be caught in the dark again!

Thea had told her she'd be eating a late dinner at the stable cafeteria and then spending the evening with Cam, so when Nancy arrived one of the grooms showed her where her cot was.

"Thanks," Nancy told him, laying out her sleeping bag.

It was cool in the barn but pleasant. The smell of hay and feed and the sharp scent of horse liniment filled the air. Nancy inhaled deeply, then stepped outside into the warm evening air.

Moonlight lit faint, ghostly strips over the ground. Her penlight safely tucked in her pocket, Nancy walked around the barns. More lights were on this evening, and there was some activity even that late. The Derby was less than forty-eight hours away, and excitement was building.

When Nancy returned to Pied Piper's stall, the grooms were already asleep, so she climbed into her sleeping bag, too. She lay awake, though, turning the mystery over in her mind.

Drugging McHugh had been a desperate act, as had been cutting the girth strap. It was clear that someone wanted McHugh out of the way, but why? Was that someone Cam? Until she knew if Johnson Farms—and Cam—inherited McHugh's seventy-five percent, Nancy had no way of knowing if Cam had a solid motive. She had to wait for her father to call back and confirm her suspicion. If there was any other motive, she couldn't think of what it was. Dollar Bill had threatened McHugh, but McHugh had promised him his money, so why would he try to kill him *before* the Derby?

Thea returned to the stable at about half past eleven. She moved quietly, but Nancy said, "I'm awake."

"Has everything been quiet around here?" Thea whispered, zipping up her sleeping bag.

"As quiet as can be expected. There's been no sign of any prowler," Nancy added.

"Well, I've got an early day tomorrow," Thea said, yawning. "Pied Piper's last workout before the race is tomorrow morning, and I want to get up and going. 'Night."

"Good night, Thea," Nancy said.

Ten minutes later she heard Thea's even breathing. Slowly, the barns settled down, and Nancy dozed off in the stillness.

She woke up later from a crick in her neck, then, remembering where she was, pulled out her penlight and took a quick look at her watch. One-thirty.

After climbing out of her sleeping bag, Nancy walked outside and stretched her legs. There were only a few lamps burning in the barns. She glanced toward Flash O'Lightnin's barn at the end of the row. It was dark and silent.

The one time Nancy had seen the shadowy figure was outside Flash's barn. Might as well make sure everything's okay down there, she thought, striding quickly across the grass.

A van rumbled into the stable area. Nancy glanced back. She could just make out Brentwood Stables in black letters across the white van.

Nancy ducked around the corner of another barn and watched the van drive by. It stopped by Flash's barn. Eddie and Ace climbed out from the cab and headed for the barn. Through the clear night air Nancy could hear them arguing.

"Handle Flash the same way in the Derby and you're out!" Eddie shouted.

"He don't like the whip," Ace answered quietly.

"Too bad! He got lazy in the last furlong, and you didn't whip him! That's not the way to win."

"If I whip him, he might go through the rail."

"If you don't," Eddie said, mimicking Ace's voice, "you won't win. . . ." His voice trailed off as they headed inside.

Nancy sighed. Ace seemed like such a straightforward guy. Why did he work for someone as obnoxious as Eddie Brent?

She crept toward their barn, interested to hear more of their conversation. Within a few feet of the entrance, she heard footsteps just ahead of her. Quickly she moved into the shadows, watching.

The outdoor lights only faintly reached this part of the stable area, but Nancy didn't want to betray herself by turning on her penlight. She squinted against the blackness and just made out someone stealing toward Flash's barn!

Swiftly and silently, Nancy followed. The figure turned around a corner of Flash's barn, and Nancy hurried after him. Not a sound reached her ears. Even Ace and Eddie seemed to have resolved their argument.

She circled the barn. The only noise was from a chorus of crickets.

Turning back, Nancy headed for the front of the barn. Here the outdoor lights offered a bit of dim light. As she hugged the side of the barn, Nancy caught sight of something small and glinting on the ground a few feet from her.

She kept the shining object in sight as she stepped away from the barn, trying to make out what it was. She'd almost reached it when she sensed someone behind her.

Nancy whipped around. She saw movement, then felt something strike her temple.

Lights exploded inside her head. I'm hit, she thought vaguely. Then, with a faint moan, she slipped to the ground, unconscious.

Chapter

Eleven

Nancy awoke to a buzzing in her ears. Her head was throbbing and her cheek burned. She slowly lifted her head and realized she was very dizzy.

"Ohhh," Nancy moaned, rolling onto her back. She inhaled several times, getting her bearings. Her head finally cleared, and she saw she was still lying on the ground, in the dark, outside Flash's barn.

Climbing to her feet, she gingerly probed her temple with her fingers. A sizable knot had formed. Someone had hit her with a hard object

—probably that rock, she thought, spying one on the ground.

Grimacing, Nancy suddenly remembered the glinting object. She walked around, searching for it, but it was gone. The person who hit me over the head must have taken it, she realized grimly. The way it had sparkled in the light reminded her of something—something she couldn't quite place right then.

"Maybe it'll come back to me later," she said aloud, wincing a little as the pain in her head increased as she started walking back to Pied Piper's barn.

There was an unusual flurry of activity in the colt's barn. It was ablaze with light and alive with loud, excited voices. Fear stabbed her. Had something happened to Pied Piper?

She ran inside and nearly collided with Thea. "What's wrong?" she asked anxiously. Then she saw Pied Piper standing in his stall, perfectly fine.

"Nancy!" Thea exclaimed. "Where were you? We were worried about you! I woke up and you were gone. When you didn't come back I was certain something had happened to you. I got Cam, and he went out searching for you. Do you know what time it is?"

Nancy glanced at her watch. It was almost three o'clock. "Pied Piper's okay, though?"

"He's fine. Where have you been?"

"Over by Flash's barn. Someone hit me over the head."

Thea's eyes widened when Nancy showed her the lump above her temple. "You need to see a doctor," Thea declared.

"It's not necessary—really," Nancy protested. "I'm fine. I just want to lie down for a while."

"I'll take you back to the hotel, then," Thea insisted. She turned to the stable boy, who looked tousled and half-asleep. "Stay awake until Cam comes back, then tell him I took Nancy home."

Thea was so determined that it was no use arguing with her, Nancy knew. Obediently she followed her out of the stable area, deciding it was best to just give in this time. She could start fresh the next day.

Sunlight streamed in the window, and Nancy opened her eyes, the effort making her head throb a little.

"Nancy?" Bess asked, her voice troubled.

Squinting, Nancy saw Bess staring down at her through worried blue eyes. "What's wrong, Bess?"

"You show up here nearly at daybreak, mumble something about someone knocking you out, then fall asleep. I should be asking you what's wrong!" Bess plopped down on the edge of Nancy's bed. "Tell me everything, Drew!"

Nancy chuckled at Bess's determined face. She told her what had happened down by Flash's barn, finishing with, "But I'm fine. I've got a pretty hard head," she added with a lopsided grin.

"You're just lucky you're okay."

"I know," Nancy said seriously. "It all happened so fast. I was just bending down to pick something up, then *wham!*" She wrinkled her nose. "The next thing I knew, I was on the ground and my head felt like I had been run over by a truck."

"Could it have been Eddie Brent or Ace?" Bess suggested. "They were both at the barn after all."

"It could have been," Nancy admitted. "But it could have been anyone else just as easily."

Bess frowned. "At least we know it wasn't Thea or Cam."

Nancy looked at her seriously. "We don't know that at all. Thea said she went to get Cam, and Cam was out looking for me. Either of them could have done it."

Bess's eyes widened. "Oh, come on, Nancy! Thea? She was so worried about you that she brought you back to the hotel."

"I know. I'm just saying we can't rule anybody out yet."

"So what was it you saw on the ground?" Bess asked after a minute.

Nancy swung her feet over the side of the bed. Her head still hurt a little bit, but she wasn't dizzy anymore. "I don't know. I feel like the answer's on the tip of my tongue, but I just haven't thought of it yet. What time is it?"

"Noon."

"Noon!" Nancy shrieked. "Come on. We've got to get to the track. This is the last day before the Derby. We've got to solve this mystery before the race. Time is running out!"

Nancy and Bess found Thea and a man they'd never met before inside Pied Piper's stall when they arrived. Thea introduced the other man as the colt's veterinarian.

"Pied Piper's listless and off his feed," Thea explained in a hushed voice to the two girls. "I'm worried sick that there's something wrong with him."

"Oh, no!" Bess cried.

"You think he's caught some kind of bug?" Nancy asked anxiously.

"I don't know. That's why Barry's here."

The veterinarian stepped out of the stall, his gaze still on the chestnut colt. "He's not running a fever," he said.

Thea's face instantly cleared. "You don't think he's sick, then?" she asked hopefully.

"I wouldn't scratch him from the race yet. Let's see how he's doing this afternoon."

After the vet left, Nancy turned to Thea. "What could be wrong with Pied Piper?"

"I'm not sure. He was fine last night, but this morning I found him like this." She gestured to the colt, whose head was hanging down. Normally Pied Piper was restless and alert. There was definitely something wrong with the colt.

"Was there any time yesterday when he was alone?" Nancy asked.

"No." Thea was positive. "There was always a stable boy here."

Remembering how tired the stable boy had looked after her accident, Nancy wondered if someone couldn't have sneaked by him the night before. Or maybe earlier in the day. Remembering Cam's angry words to Eddie Brent about drugging horses, Nancy's blood ran cold. Could Pied Piper have been given something? Maybe in his feed . . .

"Where's Pied Piper's feed?" Nancy asked.

"Right here," Thea said, gesturing to the bag of specially mixed grain.

"Let's have it analyzed and get Pied Piper some new feed from an unopened bag."

Thea's jaw dropped. "You think someone tampered with his food?"

"It's possible," Nancy said grimly as Thea hauled up the bag of grain. "There's a lot at stake here."

An hour later Nancy, Bess, and Thea had saved a sample of the feed to be analyzed, thrown out the rest, then brought in new feed. Thea talked long and hard with the stable boy. He didn't remember seeing or hearing anyone. Then she sent him to tell Cam what had happened.

Maybe I'm overreacting, Nancy thought, eyeing the Thoroughbred anxiously. Pied Piper was pretty listless, but he didn't seem to be getting any worse.

Cam stopped by Pied Piper's stall at about one-thirty. "How's he doing?" he asked Thea.

"About the same."

"I suppose you've heard about Flash," he said with a serious look on his face.

Nancy, Thea, and Bess all gazed at him blankly. "What about Flash?" Nancy asked quickly.

"He's off his feed, too, and he's sluggish and tired. Eddie's having a fit! He swears someone drugged his horse. In fact, he's accusing me."

"Oh, Cam. No!" Thea cried, her eyes wide.

"Why not?" Cam asked angrily. "It's always easy to blame me for everything, isn't it? He probably thinks I drugged Pied Piper, too!"

At that moment footsteps pounded across the barn floor as Eddie Brent burst inside. "There you are, Parker!" he snarled furiously. "Back to finish Pied Piper off, are you?"

"Watch it, Brent," Cam growled.

Before anyone could react, Brent lunged forward and seized Cam by the throat, squeezing down on his windpipe!

"You're the one trying to wipe out the competition, not me!" Cam shouted, gripping Eddie's throat as Eddie had his. "I ought to kill you right now with my bare hands!"

Chapter
Twelve

NANCY LEAPT FORWARD and grabbed one of Eddie Brent's arms. She jerked hard, loosening the enraged man's grip.

"Let go!" Eddie growled, trying to shake her off.

Cam's blue eyes blazed. He pushed Eddie away, then stood back, rubbing his throat. "You're way off base, Brent. I don't know who's responsible for Flash and Pied Piper being down, but I intend to find out!"

"Why don't you look in a mirror?" the surly owner sneered.

Cam raised his fist, ready to smash it into

Eddie's mocking face. Nancy stepped between them, intent on restoring peace.

"Cameron Parker!"

The sound of a man's voice stopped Cam cold. Nancy glanced around. It was Evan Johnson who'd spoken. He and Laura were standing just outside the barn.

Evan's face was filled with concern. "What's going on?" he asked Eddie. Eddie glared at Cam, then stomped away.

Cam lowered his fist, looking a bit self-conscious in front of Evan. "We had a disagreement," he explained. "Were you looking for me?" he added.

"Yes! There's something wrong with Toot Sweet," Evan declared, forgetting Eddie Brent in an instant. "We were doing an interview outside her stall when all of a sudden she started to droop."

"What do you mean?" Cam demanded sharply.

"The stable boy said she didn't seem a bit like herself," Laura said, slipping her arm through Cam's, her blue eyes wide and worried. "Oh, I hope nothing's wrong!"

"We said we'd come find you," Evan put in.

Cam appeared to be stunned as he took off running for Toot Sweet's stable. Evan and Laura hurried after him.

Nancy turned to Bess and Thea. "I'm going to check out Toot Sweet."

"I'm with you," said Bess.

"I'll stay with Pied Piper," Thea said grimly. "I don't want anything else to happen to him."

Nancy and Bess walked quickly toward barn eight. The crowd around the Derby favorite had swelled each day as the race grew nearer, but now, with the news about Toot Sweet's health spreading, Nancy and Bess practically had to fight their way to the filly's stable.

"Whew!" Bess declared. "This is getting crazy!"

The area around Toot Sweet's stall had been roped off, and race officials were standing guard. Nancy tried to explain that she was a friend of Cam's, but they wouldn't listen to her.

Finally Cam came outside. Cameras clicked madly, and reporters thrust microphones his way.

"Is it true that several Derby horses have been drugged, Toot Sweet among them?" one reporter burst out.

"How is the filly, Mr. Parker?" another asked.

"Will she still race?" yet another demanded.

Cam drew in a deep breath. "We don't know what's wrong. Several horses have developed symptoms of listlessness and depressed appetite.

97

Race officials are testing them for drugs. We'll know more later today."

The crowd surged in on him, the reporters clamoring for answers. Nancy and Bess were pressed back.

"I just wish I knew what was going on," Nancy muttered in frustration. Why would anyone drug all three Derby favorites? It didn't make any sense!

"Come on," she said to Bess. "Let's go have a swim at the hotel while we wait for the lab results."

Although she was trying to relax in the sun, Nancy was restless and anxious. She couldn't shake the feeling that something terrible was going to happen at the race.

Bess flipped onto her stomach, her back shiny with suntan oil. She opened one eye and glanced at Nancy, who was sitting on the end of her lounge chair. "You want to go back to the room and wait by the phone for Thea's call?"

Nancy smiled. "I think I will. Sorry. I just can't stand sunbathing this afternoon. I've got too much on my mind."

"I'll come with you," said Bess, grabbing her towel.

As soon as they stepped into their hotel room Nancy spied the flashing red light on the phone, indicating that someone had left a message. As she reached to pick up the phone to call the desk, it rang beneath her hand.

"Hello?"

"Nancy, it's Thea. The lab results just came through. Flash, Pied Piper, and Toot Sweet were all given a powerful sedative. It looks like you were right. It was in their feed."

Nancy's thoughts spun. "Someone wants all the favorites out of the race." Her mind flew to Dollar Bill. Could this be a simpler way of eliminating the competition rather than paying off jockeys to stiff a horse? Which horse, then, did Dollar Bill want to win?

"It looks like it," Thea admitted, "but they're not going to succeed. Pied Piper and Flash are doing better already."

"And Toot Sweet?"

"She still hasn't recovered. They think she was drugged later. Cam doesn't know whether to scratch her or not."

Nancy could imagine Cam's dilemma. This would be the only chance for Toot Sweet to race in the Derby, but if the horse wasn't a hundred percent, there was no way a trainer could have him—or her in this case—race.

"Thanks, Thea. We'll come back to the track right away."

Nancy pressed down on the receiver with her

finger, then dialed the desk. The first message had been from her father only a few minutes before.

"Well, I've got some of the information you wanted," Carson informed his daughter when she called him. "I talked with one of Pied Piper's other owners, Tom Marshall. Tom's an attorney in Kentucky, and I asked him to pull a few strings for me and find out the contents of Ulysses Johnson's will."

"And?" Nancy asked excitedly.

"There was a stipulation that if anything should happen to Ken McHugh, his percentage of the winnings will revert to Johnson Farms. Mr. Cameron Parker, as owner of the horses, would receive all the winnings."

Nancy drew a breath. She'd suspected as much, but to hear her suspicion stated as fact shocked her a little. Her eyes met Bess's as her father explained some of the more complicated legal terms of the will. It all boiled down to the fact that if McHugh died Cam would own one hundred percent of all the Johnson Farms horses! Except for Laura's breeding rights, the horses were virtually Cam's!

Cam had just been firmly placed at the top of Nancy's suspect list. He had the strongest motive for wanting Ken McHugh out of the way.

"Well?" Bess asked when Nancy hung up.

Nancy explained what her father had said, finishing with, "There's something that bothers me, though. Even if Cam wanted to get rid of McHugh, why would he drug his own horse? That doesn't make sense. He'd still want to win the Derby."

Bess shrugged. "But the horses are going to be okay, right? They're not out of the race yet, so drugging them didn't work."

Nancy wrinkled her nose, thinking hard. "Do you suppose Cam drugged them to throw suspicion on someone else? It's pretty risky. Or . . ."

Bess's brows lifted in expectation.

"Or maybe we're dealing with two separate crimes," Nancy theorized. "Maybe the person who tried to kill McHugh isn't the same one who drugged the horses."

"Maybe the person who tried to harm the horses will try again," Bess said.

"I don't know," Nancy said grimly. "Race officials are guarding the barns, but I want to get back to see for myself."

Nancy and Bess cut across the stable area toward Pied Piper's barn. "I don't see how anyone could get past the guards," Nancy said, looking up and down the row of barns. "But I'm still uneasy."

There was a disturbance toward the far end of

the stable yard. Eddie Brent was ranting and raving again, this time at the stable boy who was leading Flash, stretching the horse's legs.

"Eddie really knows how to win friends, doesn't he?" Bess asked sarcastically.

"Mmmm." Nancy's gaze was on Flash. The spirited colt was sleek and ready for any race. There was no evidence of listlessness.

"Flash looks great," she remarked to Bess.

"He sure does. The drugs must be wearing off."

"All the feed was changed," Nancy said. Sighing, she added, "I can't help being worried, though. Even with the guards, there's so much activity that anyone could easily sneak by unnoticed, and—"

A shout and a horse's high scream suddenly shattered the air. Hoofbeats thundered. Nancy and Bess whirled around, then froze.

Flash had reared up on his hind feet and was frantically pawing the air just over their heads!

Chapter

Thirteen

BESS SCREAMED and grabbed on to Nancy's arm. Nancy shoved her friend to one side, falling on top of her as they both tumbled to the ground.

Just as they hit the ground, Nancy felt the air whistle beside her as Flash's hooves crashed back to the hard-packed earth.

On all fours, the colt was now pounding toward the track. The shouts and screams of people scrambling out of the way followed in his wake.

"Bess! Are you all right?" Nancy asked, her voice shaking as she lifted herself up.

Bess raised her blond head. "I'm . . . okay. At

least I think so," she added, testing her right arm. Her elbow was scraped and bleeding. "What about you?"

"I'll be all right." Nancy glanced toward Flash. The colt was now galloping in frantic, tight circles, dodging several track security men and a group of stable boys and trainers. When they finally caught him, Flash kicked out with his hind feet once, then stood, snorting and pawing the ground, his flesh quivering.

"I wonder what made him take off like that?" Nancy asked out loud.

Eddie Brent and Ace Hanford reached them just then, breathing hard from their run. "Filthy, pigheaded monster," Brent raged, glaring at Flash.

Ace pretended not to know Nancy, but he said quietly, "He might be all those things, but he's a fast one."

Brent nodded curtly to Nancy and Bess as he stalked toward the nervous colt. It was his only apology for the near accident.

Ace glanced back at Nancy and Bess. "Glad you weren't hurt," he said softly, then followed after Flash's owner.

As Bess and Nancy walked back to Pied Piper's stall, Bess asked, "Why does Ace put up with that awful Mr. Brent?"

"Good question," Nancy murmured. She watched as the jockey grabbed Flash's bridle, calmly walking the terrified horse around, cooling him down.

"Come on, Bess," Nancy said to her friend. "Let's get out of here." Bess nodded in relief, and the two friends headed back to Pied Piper's stall.

Thea hadn't seen Flash's escape, but she'd heard about it from the excited stable boys. Nancy filled her in on the details of their part in the incident.

"You could have been killed!" Thea gasped. "Flash is one of the most dangerous Thoroughbreds here."

"I know," Bess agreed with feeling, examining the bandage Thea was going to wrap around her elbow.

"Eddie Brent is so cheap!" Thea declared. "He won't hire enough stable boys and grooms to take care of Flash. Ace has to do everything, and it's too much for him sometimes. Like today . . . Flash broke away. If Eddie would just spend money where it counts—" She stopped short, her eyes flashing.

"Why does Ace put up with Eddie?" Nancy asked.

Thea's mouth tightened. "For the horses, I guess. Eddie has winners. Ace has ridden for a lot of owners, and he wins the most on Eddie's horses. A lot of jockeys would put up with Eddie's tantrums just to ride a horse like Flash.

"With all his success, though, Eddie doesn't understand a horse's mentality," Thea went on. "For instance, Flash works better without the whip, but Eddie won't listen to Ace."

"Brent seems to like to do things his way," Nancy murmured. Remembering that Cam in anger had said Brent would drug horses, Nancy now wondered if the accusations could be true. Brent was thoroughly unlikable. Cam might have a strong motive to kill McHugh, but Brent might have an even stronger motive to eliminate the competition.

Except that Flash was drugged, too.

Nancy was still mulling that over later in the afternoon while she and Bess watched the day's races from the infield homestretch rail. The crowd's excitement was reaching a peak. As the Derby grew closer, Nancy could feel the excitement building. By the next day, when the Derby horses reached the gate, the crowd would be well over a hundred thousand.

"Let's go inside the clubhouse for a bite to eat," Nancy suggested to Bess as the last race finished.

The crowd was dispersing as Nancy and Bess

entered the main clubhouse building. From the direction of Skye Terrace—the exclusive glass-enclosed seating area dubbed Millionaire's Row —Evan and Laura Johnson appeared. Laura once again wore her mink coat, and teardrop diamond earrings twinkled at her ears.

Seeing Nancy and Bess, Evan boomed out jovially, "Well, if it isn't Miss Drew and Miss Marvin. We were just coming to the barns to find you."

"You were?" Bess asked, surprised.

"As Pied Piper's representative owners, I wondered if you might join us at a party at our home this evening. I intend to invite Thea, too, of course. There'll be other owners and trainers there as well."

Mention of Thea brought a sulky look to Laura's mouth, but then she quickly hid it behind a smile. "Cam will be there also," she added.

"We'd be happy to join you," Nancy accepted. "Thanks for the invitation."

"Good. Good." Evan nodded and pulled a card from a thick leather wallet. "This is the address." He handed the card to Nancy. Tucking Laura's arm through his, he led her toward the door, calling back, "We'll see you around seven, then."

"You think Walt will be there?" Bess asked excitedly as soon as Evan and Laura disappeared through the door.

"He is Toot Sweet's jockey, so I'd bet on it." Nancy's eyes followed Evan and Laura's progress down the steps. "I wonder if this party will be as eventful as the last," she murmured thoughtfully.

"I hope not," Bess said, steering her friend into the clubhouse restaurant. "I think it's about time we had some plain old southern-style fun. Isn't that why we came here in the first place?"

Nancy laughed and shook her head. "Okay, Bess, I get the point. Tonight we take a break from detecting." Bess gave her friend a skeptical look. Nancy put out her hand to shake Bess's. "I promise!"

The Johnson home was at the end of a long oak-lined drive about fifteen miles outside Louisville. White columns rose two full stories, and a wide porch extended across the face of the house. Two huge brass lamps flanked the front double doors.

"I feel like I've stepped back in time a century," Bess murmured, gazing at the house and the miles of fence rails that stretched over the hills, gleaming snow-white in the moonlight.

Nancy glanced at the other cars outside Evan

Johnson's home. There were only a handful of people there. Eddie Brent would undoubtedly be left off the guest list, Nancy thought, remembering the rivalry between the Kentucky breeders and the surly California horse owner.

"How do I look?" Bess asked as they walked up the front stone steps.

"Terrific as always," Nancy replied absently. She gazed past the house to the fields beyond. No horses were in sight.

"You didn't even look!" Bess complained.

Nancy glanced at Bess's sky blue silk dress. It hugged her curves and made her blue eyes shine. Her hair was floating freely around her shoulders.

"You look mahvelous," Nancy drawled. "Simply mahvelous."

"My bangs are at least bearable now." Bess giggled. "You look mahvelous, too."

Nancy had pulled her reddish blond hair into a french braid. Her dress was blue, too, but it was a dark midnight shade, and the satiny material whispered as she walked. Around her throat was a rope of pearls.

"If we go to any more parties, I'm sunk," Nancy remarked. "I don't have another dress."

"We could trade," Bess pointed out.

"Oh, sure!" Since Bess was several inches

shorter, Nancy laughed aloud. "Do you know what I'd look like in—that?" She pointed to Bess's dress.

"I guess it was just wishful thinking, huh?" Bess agreed, glancing wistfully at Nancy's gown.

They both laughed as the door opened, and a butler dressed in a formal black suit invited them into the house. He escorted them straight down a long, narrow hallway to the backyard. Nancy would have liked to explore the immense house, but most of the doors were closed. The brief glimpses she had inside some of the open rooms were a bit disappointing. She'd expected the decor to be right out of a glossy magazine, but most of the furniture looked old, massive, and a little worn.

The back porch and large sloping yard were lit by strings of colored lights, artfully arranged overhead in a fan-shaped design. A white fence glowed beneath misty rainbow colors. Beyond the fence stood a building that Nancy guessed was once the Johnson family's well-stocked barn and stables. Now it looked empty and dark and faintly menacing. Nancy wondered where the horses were kept.

Spying Walt, Bess made a beeline toward where the blond jockey stood, looking slightly uncomfortable in his tuxedo.

Nancy was about to search out Thea when Evan Johnson suddenly appeared at her elbow. "Miss Drew!" he greeted her expansively. "You must have some punch." He gestured to an ornate silver bowl on a table to one side.

"Thank you," Nancy said.

As she went to get the punch, she glanced around. Wow, she thought to herself, noticing the large serving staff and elegant serving trays covered with all kinds of delicious-smelling entrees. Evan had spared no expense.

And yet . . .

Nancy's gaze traveled up the back of the house. There were signs of neglect: the house needed painting, a rail around an upper balcony bowed out unsafely, flower boxes had been raked out and never replanted.

Why is Evan Johnson letting his house go like this? Nancy wondered as she served herself a glass of the fruity iced punch. Most people with his wealth and social connections would keep up their property for appearances' sake if nothing else.

"Nancy!" Bess waved to Nancy to join her and Walt.

Walt's normally cheerful face was serious. He was the only jockey at the party.

"Is something wrong?" Nancy asked him.

"No. I just didn't want to come," he admitted. "This isn't my kind of thing, but Evan invited me, and Cam thought that since I'm riding Toot Sweet I ought to come." He tugged on his collar. "So here I am."

"I'm glad you're here," Bess told him, her eyes twinkling. "I need someone to tell me what I can and can't eat!"

"Stay away from that vegetable dip," Walt said seriously. "It looks good, but it's loaded with fat. I asked the caterers when I was in the kitchen."

"You were in the kitchen?" Nancy asked, amused by Walt's obsession with a proper diet.

"I mixed a special health drink," he confessed, lifting a crystal glass which held a strange, dark purple mixture. "There's more in the refrigerator if you want some."

"Could I have a taste?" Bess asked bravely.

Walt brightened. "Sure. Come on." He led her toward the kitchen. Bess glanced back once, and Nancy clutched her throat, pretending to choke.

"Better you than me, Bess." Nancy laughed softly to herself and headed over to Cam and Thea's table. On the way, Laura Johnson intercepted her.

"So, how are you enjoying the party?" Laura asked politely.

"It's great. I haven't had a chance to sample much of the food yet, but I'm on my way."

Laura wasn't really listening. Her gaze was on Cam. "Mmmm. That's nice."

Nancy bit her bottom lip, thinking hard. This was a perfect opportunity to ask a few questions. "I understand Cam actually owns Toot Sweet," she said innocently, sipping her punch.

Laura whipped around as if her head had been pulled by a string. "Who told you that? Cam?"

"Thea."

Color swept up Laura's neck. "Well, it's true. Daddy and I don't really own Toot Sweet. We've never been that interested in racing. But this house is ours," she said firmly, as if Nancy had questioned it. "U.J. might have left Johnson Farms to Cam, but he left me the house. It's been in the family for generations. Johnson Farms, where the horses are stabled, is much newer. It's on the other end of Louisville." She waved vaguely toward the north.

Cam and Thea rose from their table, and Laura hurried over to them. The poor girl seemed oblivious to the fact that Cam cared for Thea. Both Cam and Thea excused themselves as soon as Laura joined them—Thea headed into the house.

As Nancy watched Thea's retreat, Eddie Brent suddenly appeared on the porch. Evan Johnson walked stiffly toward him with his hand extended. Both men's jaws were clenched tight.

Cam appeared at Nancy's side then. "Hard to believe, isn't it?" he remarked. "I guess he decided he couldn't deliberately leave Eddie out."

This was the perfect opportunity to talk to Cam alone, Nancy thought. "I've been wanting to talk to you about Ken McHugh," she said.

"He's still in a coma," Cam answered, anticipating her question.

"I know." Nancy drew a breath. "Actually, it was something else I wanted to ask." She paused for a moment, then dove in, trying to make her question sound as innocent as possible. "Why was McHugh going to ride Toot Sweet in the Derby? I mean, Thea told me you own Johnson Farms, and you didn't seem to get along with McHugh. Why didn't you choose Walt?"

"What are you getting at?" Cam demanded, his eyes narrowing. "McHugh's a good jockey, and he knows Toot Sweet better than Walt. I still wish he were riding in the Derby."

With that, Cam walked back to his table, putting a quick end to Nancy's questions.

Dinner was served outside, and Nancy was seated with Bess and Laura and Walt. Laura kept casting wistful glances at Cam, but he had eyes only for Thea, who was sitting next to him at a small, two-person table.

After dinner Walt went to talk to Cam, and

Nancy and Bess had a few moments alone. "I took one sip of Walt's special drink and I couldn't drink any more," Bess admitted. "I poured the rest out behind a bush when he wasn't looking. It had all kinds of terrible things in it, like wheat germ and whey and gelatin. Yuck!" She shuddered.

Nancy glanced at Walt. One of the caterers was bringing him another glass of his drink. "Well, he seems to like it."

Cam and Thea left a few moments later and Laura abruptly disappeared into the house. Eddie Brent, who had been standing on the porch alone, glowered, then turned on his heel and left.

"Looks like the party's ending," Bess said.

"Let's say good night to Evan and leave, too," suggested Nancy.

Walt returned to their table and said to Bess, somewhat reluctantly, "I think I'd better go home. I don't know what's wrong with me, but I feel sort of tired."

"That's okay," Bess told him affectionately. "We can celebrate after the Derby tomorrow."

Walt, Bess, and Nancy all said good night to Evan then walked through the shadowed hallway to the front porch. Going down the steps, Walt suddenly stumbled, clutching at one of the columns. He started to gasp.

Bess looked at him in alarm. "Walt! Are you all right?"

Nancy was beside him. "What's wrong?"

"I—don't know! I feel dizzy. Weak. I think it's—" Then, without another word, the jockey pitched forward down the steps and sprawled on the ground, unconscious.

Chapter

Fourteen

"WALT!" BESS SHRIEKED, kneeling beside him.

"Quick! Loosen his tie!" Nancy cried, her fingers already performing the task.

"He's breathing!" Bess cried in relief.

Walt's chest rose and fell slowly, but the jockey was out cold.

"I'll go back inside and call an ambulance. Stay with him," Nancy told her friend.

Inside the house the first person she saw was a caterer. "Do you know where a phone is?"

"There's one in the kitchen," he answered, eyeing her dubiously.

"It's an emergency," she explained, already in

117

motion. "Find Evan Johnson and tell him I'm calling an ambulance for Walt!"

Inside the kitchen Nancy found the phone, dialed 911, and explained about Walt. She was just hanging up when Evan burst into the kitchen.

"What are you doing?" he asked. "What's going on?"

"It's Walt Collins," Nancy quickly explained. "He started gasping, then fell down the steps and passed out."

"What?" Evan was astounded. "Is he all right?"

"I don't know. He complained about being tired, then he just collapsed," Nancy answered. "Maybe it was something he ate," she said almost to herself.

Evan stared at Nancy as she started to sweep past him back toward Walt. "What are you suggesting?" he asked, worried, following on her heels.

"Just that Walt may have eaten something that didn't agree with him. I don't know. We'll soon find out in any case. The paramedics are on their way."

Several of the other guests had gathered on the porch, watching Walt anxiously. Bess was still kneeling beside him. Walt's color was gray, and his breathing was shallow and ragged.

"The ambulance will be here soon," Nancy assured Bess.

"I want to go to the hospital with him."

Nancy nodded. "Me, too."

As Evan gazed down at Walt, his forehead wrinkled with lines of distress. In the distance the wail of a siren sounded, and through the trees Nancy could periodically see the flashing red and white lights of the ambulance coming in their direction.

Hang in there, Walt, Nancy thought. Help is on its way.

"Poisoned?" Bess repeated in a hushed tone almost an hour later. "Walt was poisoned?"

"Not poisoned exactly. He ingested an overdose of some sedative," Nancy explained, also in a low voice. Grabbing Bess by the arm, she led her away from the emergency room. "I overheard the doctors talking. They've pumped his stomach and given him something to counteract the sedative."

"Will he be—"

"Yes," Nancy assured her swiftly. "He's going to be fine. Listen, Bess, McHugh was given a heavy dose of sedatives right before the race. I'll bet you anything this is the same type! Someone's trying to wipe out Toot Sweet's jockeys and keep the filly from racing!"

Bess's mouth dropped open. "But she'll still race, won't she?"

"I'm sure Cam can get her another jockey if Walt isn't well enough in time."

"Nancy, who's behind this?" Bess cried angrily.

"That's what we're trying to find out. Bess, what did Walt eat at the party?"

Bess drew a deep breath and collected herself, thinking hard. "Hardly anything. Nothing that had fat or preservatives or artificial color. He had some of the rice, but so did I, and he had a couple of chicken wings, I think."

"He did drink his special concoction," Nancy added.

"So did I," Bess answered.

Nancy met her gaze. "Only one sip."

"You think someone spiked his drink?" Bess asked, horrified.

"It's the only answer I can come up with. If the sedative had been in something he'd eaten before the party, it probably would have showed up sooner." Nancy propelled Bess toward the door. "I've got to get that pitcher and have the contents tested."

"You mean we're going back to Evan Johnson's house?"

"Whoever did this, Bess, is going to try to

cover it up as soon as possible. We've got to get back there before it's too late!"

The lights were blazing as they pulled up in front of the Johnsons' graceful southern mansion. The catering staff's minivan was still parked near the kitchen, and the helpers were packing away the portable chairs and tables.

Nancy and Bess circled the house and entered by the kitchen door. The kitchen was spotless, with the counters gleaming. Opening the refrigerator, Nancy's worst fears were confirmed. There was no pitcher inside.

"Do you remember what it looked like?" she asked Bess.

"It was clear plastic. Kind of square."

Nancy checked in the sink. The pitcher was there, rinsed out and awaiting the dishwasher.

"What are you doing here?" Evan Johnson asked in such a loud voice that Bess gasped.

Even Nancy's heart lurched at his sharp tone. "This is the pitcher that contained Walt's special drink."

Evan blinked. "And?"

"I think someone laced it with a powerful sedative, maybe even enough to kill him," Nancy told him evenly. She explained what she'd overheard from the doctors at the hospital.

Evan stared at her—hard. "Don't you think

we should leave these outlandish theories to the authorities, Ms. Drew?"

"Nancy's a detective," Bess declared proudly as Laura joined them in the kitchen. "Really. She's solved lots of cases. And with Ken McHugh being drugged in a similar way, her theory's not so outlandish, is it?"

Nancy watched powerful emotions play across Evan's face, but most of all he seemed to be in shock. When Laura had walked into the kitchen, he had glanced at her blankly, barely seeing her.

Laura appeared to be thunderstruck still. "A detective?" she repeated, swinging her head to stare at the pitcher in Nancy's hands, her diamond earrings gently rocking. She was frightened.

She knows something! Nancy thought with barely suppressed excitement.

"This is terrible," Evan muttered, rubbing his hands together nervously. "Someone's trying to make me look bad."

"You?" Nancy asked.

"Well, this happened at my home, didn't it? To Toot Sweet's jockey! First McHugh, and now Walt. It doesn't make any sense, unless . . ." He sucked in a breath, his eyes narrowing. "Unless that scoundrel Brent's behind it!"

"Eddie Brent?" asked Nancy.

"You should have never invited him!" Laura

suddenly cried. "I knew it. He'd do anything to win, and he hates Cam!"

"I had to invite him," Evan said, almost apologetically. "The man's a talented breeder, and people respect him. That's just the way it is."

Laura responded with stony silence.

"Do you think we should take this to the police?" Bess asked, indicating the pitcher.

"Yes. There might be traces of the sedative left," Nancy agreed.

Laura stepped forward, almost involuntarily. For one tense moment Nancy thought she was going to try to yank the pitcher from her grasp. But then Laura stepped back, her pretty face set and serious.

As if feeling Nancy's eyes on her, Laura glanced away. The diamond earrings sparkled and twinkled. In a flash, Nancy realized why she couldn't take her eyes off them.

One of those very same earrings had been lying on the ground outside Flash's stall last night when she was attacked!

Chapter

Fifteen

Nᴀɴᴄʏ'ꜱ ɢᴀᴢᴇ ɴᴇᴠᴇʀ ʟᴇꜰᴛ the girl's face. Was Laura the one who'd knocked her over the head?

She kept her cool. If Laura had been outside Flash's stall that night, the girl could be dangerous. She tried to keep her voice calm and even.

"Well, I guess there's nothing to do but wait to hear how Walt's doing," Nancy remarked, keeping a tight hold on the pitcher. "If he can't ride tomorrow, will Toot Sweet still race?"

"That's entirely up to Cam," Evan responded distractedly.

"Come on, Bess," Nancy said, urging her friend toward the door.

"Wait a minute." Evan stopped her. His skin was pale and he looked shaken, but his mouth was set determinedly. "I'll take the pitcher over to the police right now. If what you say is true, I want to talk to them myself."

"Daddy!" Laura cried involuntarily.

"What?" he demanded, irritated.

Laura's mouth worked but no words came out.

Nancy watched this exchange with interest. What was going on between the two of them? "I'd like to come with you to the police station," Nancy told him.

Evan frowned and sighed. "Ms. Drew, with all due respect, I'd like to go by myself. This happened at my house, and though I'm sure you're a talented detective, I know one member of the force personally and would rather see him alone. Do you understand?"

Johnson was concerned about appearances, Nancy realized. He wanted to keep Walt's accident as quiet as possible in case it reflected poorly on him.

"Would you let me know what happens?" she asked.

"I'll call you in the morning," he agreed, nodding.

"Daddy," Laura said again, clutching at his sleeve as Nancy handed over the pitcher.

"Laura, stay out of this," he said flatly, heading

125

for the door. Nancy and Bess followed him outside. Laura didn't move. Instead, she remained frozen to her spot, looking scared to death.

"What's going on with Laura?" Bess asked as she and Nancy followed Evan's car on the way back into Louisville. "She's acting so strange."

"I know." Nancy chewed on her bottom lip. "Remember that object I saw glinting outside Flash's barn? It was Laura Johnson's earring. I'm sure of it now!"

"Her earring!" Bess echoed, blinking rapidly.

Nancy nodded. "I have a vague memory that I might have interrupted Laura tampering with the feed."

"But why?" Bess demanded.

"Maybe she doesn't want Toot Sweet to race," Nancy said slowly, putting her thoughts into words. "Maybe that's why McHugh and Walt were given the sedatives."

"But that doesn't make sense!" Bess argued. "Why drug Flash and Pied Piper if all she cared about was Toot Sweet being scratched from the race? And why does she want Toot Sweet scratched? She owns the breeding rights to her, and a win at the Derby makes the filly much more valuable."

Nancy frowned. "I don't know what to say. But I think there's more at work here than just Laura.

Drugging Pied Piper and Flash only makes sense if whoever did it *did* want Toot Sweet to race." Nancy shook her head, trying to clear her thoughts. "You know, Toot Sweet was drugged later, maybe as an afterthought. Do you suppose that was a cover-up?" She frowned. "That doesn't make sense. Toot Sweet still might win."

"It's so confusing," Bess said with a sigh.

"And why drug the jockeys?" Nancy mused aloud. "What has that got to do with anything?" Taking a deep breath, she added, "Oh, Bess, the answers are all there. I'm sure of it. I just don't know what they are."

"So what now?" asked Bess.

"Back to the hotel for some rest. It's late and tomorrow's Derby day. The horses are fine, and as long as Walt feels okay by race time, the race is on for all three favorites."

The phone woke Nancy from strange dreams in which she was haunted by horses thundering down a track covered with dollar bills. Evan, Laura, and Cam's faces appeared from time to time in misty fragments. McHugh was alive and grinning. Thea stood by, silent and worried. Nancy's mind even conjured up a picture of U.J., an old man standing by the rail with a piece of paper crumpled in his fist—his will.

Nancy lifted one eyelid as the phone jangled

again. She groped for the receiver, glancing at the clock. It was barely six o'clock in the morning.

"Hello?"

"Ms. Drew?" It was Evan Johnson's voice.

Nancy bolted upright in bed, all traces of sleep gone. "Yes?"

"You were right about the pitcher. The police found traces of a powerful sedative. The dose could have killed Walt if he hadn't gotten to the hospital in time." Evan's voice sounded incredibly weary, as if he couldn't believe what he was saying. "Who could have done such a thing?"

"Who is it?" Bess asked sleepily from her bed.

Nancy mouthed Evan Johnson's name. Bess's eyebrows lifted.

Nancy was debating about telling Evan her suspicions about Laura, when Evan suddenly said, "Ms. Drew, you said you were a detective. If you've got any idea who's behind this, I'd like to know who it is."

"I don't know how yet exactly, or why, but I think your daughter may be involved, Mr. Johnson," Nancy responded soberly. To Evan's cry of protest, she added, "Let me explain," and launched into the story about the earring.

There was silence when she finished. Nancy felt sorry for Evan. The news must have shattered him.

"I would like to talk to you," Evan said, his

voice strained. "But not over the phone. I think I have some information that may help you."

"Let's meet somewhere," Nancy suggested, positive she was now on the trail of the solution to the mystery.

"Come to the house. Laura's not here."

"We'll be there right away," Nancy assured him.

"We?"

"Is it all right if I bring Bess with me?"

He hesitated, then said, "Just don't bring anyone else. Please. This is personal. And, Miss Drew?"

"Yes?"

"Hurry," he said simply before hanging up.

Evan Johnson's house appeared to be deserted in the late-morning light. Bess wrinkled her nose. "Aren't there any servants working here?"

"Probably not. The Johnsons don't have the money they'd like everyone to think they have." Nancy told her about the signs of neglect she'd noticed the night before. "Laura could have had that mink a long time," she added thoughtfully. "I bet those diamonds are fakes!"

"Oh, Nancy, I think you're right," Bess said excitedly.

Nancy narrowed her eyes as she worked out an idea. "Laura said U.J. willed her the house, but this place is a white elephant. Think of the maintenance costs! I don't think they can keep it up. The only way they'll get any money is if they sell, and that would kill them socially. Everyone would find out they'd been living beyond their means. I suspect they might even be on the brink of bankruptcy."

"So, maybe Laura drugged Flash and Pied Piper so Toot Sweet would be assured of winning," Bess concluded, warming to the theme. Her pretty face clouded. "Then who drugged Toot Sweet?"

"And who wanted to do away with the filly's jockeys?" Nancy added, winking at Bess as she slipped out of the car and headed up the front steps.

"You sound like you have an idea!" Bess exclaimed. "Come on, Nan. Give!"

Nancy knocked on the heavy double doors. "I haven't got it all worked out yet, but I'm almost positive we're dealing with two separate cases." She counted on her fingers. "One, Laura Johnson wants Toot Sweet to win because she owns the breeding rights to the filly. The more the filly races and wins, the more valuable her offspring will be. Therefore she drugged the two closest competitors."

"And the other case?" Bess asked excitedly.

Nancy rapped on the door again, wondering

what was taking Evan so long. "Someone drugged Toot Sweet's jockeys, and Laura can't be doing that. She'd have no reason." Nancy chewed on her lower lip. "It does seem like someone really wanted to get McHugh. First the girth strap was cut, and then he was drugged."

"So why was Walt drugged?"

Nancy shrugged. "Maybe to throw suspicion off whoever was after McHugh." She frowned at the door, testing the handle. "Where's Evan?" she asked.

Bess shook her head, baffled. "You don't suppose something happened to him, do you?" she asked anxiously.

Before Nancy could answer, the sound of a gunshot shattered the still morning air!

Chapter

Sixteen

"COME ON, BESS!" Nancy cried, running around the side of the house in the direction of the gunshot.

"Be careful, Nan," Bess shouted as she chased after her.

The back grounds of the house were empty. Nancy stopped short, glancing around. Her gaze stopped on the stables. Something was wrong. The door was open.

"Bess, look!" Nancy grabbed Bess's arm. "Someone's inside the stables!"

"Someone with a gun," Bess reminded her, swallowing hard.

"I'm going to check it out. Evan could be in trouble. You can stay here and—"

"No!" Bess shook her head adamantly. "I'm coming with you."

Nancy gave her loyal friend a warm smile. "Come on, then."

They ran quietly across the grass and through the back gate. The stables looked as though they'd been empty for years. Nancy crept inside the door. Morning sunshine filtered in through dust-thickened cracks. Stale air filled Nancy's nostrils. A quick glance told her there was no one inside.

"The place looks deserted," Bess whispered, following Nancy inside. She huddled close to her friend's side.

Movement caught Nancy's eye. A scythe, hung on the far wall at the end of the stalls, was gently swinging back and forth. Had someone bumped it? She squeezed Bess's arm to stop her from talking and pointed to the rocking scythe. Bess's blue eyes widened.

Nancy crept forward, careful to be as quiet as possible. Bess followed close behind. They were halfway down the row of stalls when the door behind them was suddenly slammed shut!

"Nancy!" Bess cried.

Nancy whirled around and raced back. She

yanked on the handle, but the door wouldn't budge. It was locked tight.

Hearing running footsteps, Nancy called out. But the footsteps just ran on.

"We're locked in," she said to Bess. "Someone did this on purpose. Someone who knew we were coming here!"

"Evan?" Bess asked, her voice quavering.

"He's the most likely suspect." Nancy was grim. "Wait!" Nancy sniffed and her blue eyes widened. She caught the distinct scent of lighter fluid and burning wood.

Bess screamed. "The stables are on fire!"

Nancy whipped around. From the outside wall, a crackle of flames was followed by a wave of thick, choking smoke. Heat blasted toward Nancy, scorching her face. Whoever had locked them in had set the barn on fire!

"We've got to find something to smash through the door!" she cried, her gaze darting feverishly around the dilapidated stables.

Bess coughed and pulled the bottom of her shirt from the waistband of her shorts, holding it to her mouth.

Nancy ran to the wall where the scythe was hanging. Seconds counted. If she didn't hurry they would both die!

She grabbed the scythe, then hurried back to

the barn door. Bess hadn't moved; her eyes were round with fear.

Nancy shoved her shoulder against the door and pushed, trying to break the lock with her weight. The wood groaned, but the door remained locked and in place.

Hefting the scythe, Nancy hurled it at the door with all her might. The wood splintered beside the lock with a loud crack. A small hole opened. Nancy gulped in fresh air, then slammed the scythe against the door once again. With a last squeal of metal the padlock on the outside broke free, and she and Bess tumbled into the sunshine.

They ran far from the burning stables, both girls coughing and choking. By now flames were licking at the roof. Nancy and Bess stood still, gulping in lungfuls of fresh air.

"What are you doing here?" a stern voice called out.

Nancy looked up. A policeman was standing in front of her, staring at her as if she were a criminal!

"We were caught in the barn. We just escaped," Nancy explained. A wave of relief passed over her as she heard the far-off wail of a fire engine.

"Come with me," the stern-faced policeman ordered. "You, too," he said to Bess.

"We need to get to a phone," Nancy protested.

"Someone tried to kill us! We were supposed to meet Evan Johnson here. This is his home, but then we heard a gunshot, and—"

"Save it for Lieutenant Masterson," the policeman ordered. "You can tell him the whole story at the station."

"The station!" Nancy echoed in amazement. "You're taking us in? On what charge?"

His gaze was cold. "Vandalism and arson," he said flatly.

Nancy was shocked. She tried to tell him that he was wasting time, but the policeman wouldn't listen. The officer ordered her and Bess into the backseat of a police cruiser and quickly drove them to the Louisville police station.

Lieutenant Masterson was a tall, thin man with red hair and a no-nonsense attitude. "Are these the vandals?" he asked the policeman who'd brought Nancy and Bess in.

"Yes, sir."

"Vandals?" Nancy couldn't believe her ears. "We didn't vandalize anything! We were set up!"

Nancy stared at the lieutenant, her chin determined. Someone must have tipped the police off. How else had they gotten to Evan Johnson's so fast?

"How did you know about the burning stables?" Nancy demanded, watching Lieutenant Masterson's face closely.

"We had an anonymous phone tip," he admitted.

"An anonymous phone call. Someone called and *told* you the stables were burning?"

"We were informed that vandals had started a fire."

Nancy blinked several times, her mind racing. "Was it a man who called?" she asked. When Lieutenant Masterson nodded, she added soberly, "It must have been Evan Johnson. He was the only person who knew where we would be."

Lieutenant Masterson cleared his throat and said dryly, "Ms. Drew, realize what you're saying. Mr. Johnson is a respected member of this community."

"Who may be a criminal," Nancy said tersely.

"Do you have any proof to substantiate your claims?"

"He locked us in the stables and left us to die!" Bess cried in disbelief. "What more proof do you need?"

"He was going to bring in a pitcher," Nancy put in, her words tumbling over one another in alarm as she realized she'd been duped by Evan. She quickly explained about Walt's drink being drugged. "Did he bring a pitcher in? He said he was going to have it tested for drugs."

Lieutenant Masterson frowned. "No pitcher

was brought in to my knowledge, but let me make a call."

While the lieutenant checked with the crime lab, Nancy glanced anxiously at the clock on the wall behind his desk. The minutes were ticking away. It was already two o'clock! Somehow she had to convince Masterson they needed to chase down Evan and Laura Johnson before it was too late!

She realized now that Evan and Laura must have been working together—and it probably was all because of money. They must be near bankruptcy to be so desperate. That's why one of them—probably Laura—had drugged both Pied Piper and Flash. She and Evan wanted both horses out of the race. Then they gave Toot Sweet a much lighter dose to throw suspicion off them.

"No one brought in a pitcher for testing," Lieutenant Masterson said. He looked a little confused, as if he were finally starting to believe Nancy and Bess were innocent victims.

"Walt Collins was drugged last night," Nancy said, hammering her point home. "Ken McHugh was drugged a few days ago. Someone's done it on purpose, and I'm almost certain it had to be Evan Johnson and his daughter, Laura."

"Maybe you should start at the beginning," Lieutenant Masterson suggested.

Once again Nancy glanced at the clock. Quickly and concisely, she brought the lieutenant up to date, telling him everything she'd learned over the past week. She told him about Dollar Bill, U.J.'s will, Evan and Laura's probable need for cash, and even her suspicions about Cameron Parker and Eddie Brent. Finally she pleaded, "We've got to get to the racetrack! Come with me and I'll prove I'm right!"

"Okay." Masterson nodded. His attitude had changed. Nancy realized that she'd convinced him that she was no criminal and that she needed help.

"There are too many things that have happened that don't add up," he told her. "At the very least, Mr. Johnson owes us an explanation. Let's go."

Nancy and Bess followed the lieutenant out to one of the patrol cars. She and Bess and another officer climbed into the back seat. Lieutenant Masterson and a third officer settled themselves in the front. Lights flashing and siren wailing, Masterson drove them toward the racetrack.

Nancy sat on the edge of her seat. Derby post time was five-thirty! How would they ever find Evan Johnson in the huge crowd?

"Oh, I wish I knew that Walt was okay!" Bess moaned as they sped through a now-deserted Louisville. Everyone was at Churchill Downs. "Do you think Walt'll be riding Toot Sweet?"

"Let's hope so," Nancy said grimly.

The officer sitting in the front passenger seat craned his neck, turning to look at them in horror. "Not racing? Toot Sweet is the filly of the decade! She's got to race!"

The filly of the decade. Thoughts clicked in place in Nancy's mind, like the tumblers of a lock. Toot Sweet *was* the filly of the decade. She'd received national attention. She was a newsmaker. With Ken McHugh's and Walt's attempted murders, the filly was an even bigger story! Her fame had undoubtedly grown outside of racing circles.

In fact, Nancy realized, if Toot Sweet won the Derby, she would be famous. Laura Johnson, as owner of Toot Sweet's breeding rights, would have other owners pounding on her door, begging to breed their stallions to Toot Sweet.

"I think I just figured out why Walt was drugged," Nancy murmured, explaining how the extra publicity would help the Johnsons.

But why McHugh? she asked herself.

Churchill Downs was a madhouse. Traffic was jammed for miles around the track and even the police couldn't get through. After fifteen minutes of barely moving, Lieutenant Masterson said, "Come on, let's go." With that, they all climbed out of the car and ran to the grandstand gates.

Nancy, Bess, and the officers stuck together, fighting their way through the crowds to the stables.

Nancy recognized a heavyset man arguing with one of the other Derby jockeys in the stable area. Grabbing Lieutenant Masterson's arm, she cried, "That's Dollar Bill—the bookie I heard threatening Ken McHugh."

"Come on!" Lieutenant Masterson ordered the other two officers. "Let's get him."

Dollar Bill glanced up, saw the lieutenant and his men, and pushed the jockey toward them, blocking the officers' way. The bookie zigzagged toward the main grandstand, shoving people out of his way.

Nancy grabbed Bess's arm. "Let's look for Evan and Laura. I'm sure they're both here. Evan thinks he's gotten rid of us, so he probably feels safe."

"Where could they be?" Bess asked. "We've searched the grandstands and the stable area."

Nancy glanced toward the clubhouse. Skye Terrace. Millionaire's Row. "It's almost post time, Bess. They must already be seated. Come on!"

Nancy practically pulled Bess through the crowds as they headed for the outdoor stairs to the exclusive seating area.

A burly security guard stood halfway up the steps, guarding the glass-enclosed seating area. Nancy rushed up to him. "I've got to speak to someone inside." she explained. "It's an emergency!"

"Yes, ma'am. It always is," he answered in a sour voice.

"No, really. I have to find someone. It's important." *A matter of life or death!* was on the tip of her tongue, but she knew he wouldn't believe her if she said it.

"Sorry, ma'am. No one enters without a ticket."

Bess tugged at Nancy's sleeve. "The horses are walking to the gate!" she cried.

The guard glanced over his shoulder, and Nancy took advantage of his lapse to dart around him, taking the stairs two at a time. Shouts and screams filled the air. The crowd was roaring, cheering for their favorites.

At the top of the stairs Nancy was reaching for the doorknob as the door opened.

Laura Johnson stepped into the door frame and stopped short right in front of Nancy. Her eyes filled with shock. "You're alive!"

"That's right," Nancy said grimly.

With a scream, Laura ran past her and down the stairs, her shoulder bumping Nancy's. Nancy stumbled, losing her balance and landing against the stair rail.

Suddenly she was slipping backward over the rail. Her hand reached out, clutching for a hold, but grabbed only air.

It was no use! She was going to fall fifty feet onto the crowd below!

Chapter

Seventeen

Nancy's arm flailed out one last time and she hooked the rail with her right elbow. She was dangling from one arm now. Closing her eyes, she willed her racing heart to slow down. The crowd's screams filled her ears.

"Nancy!" Bess's frightened voice sounded above all the noise.

Arm aching, Nancy gritted her teeth and swung her free hand around, grappling for a hold with it. Her fingers connected with the rail and she hung panting, facing the stairs.

Opening her eyes, she looked up. Bess was reaching over the rail, struggling to reach her.

Then a young man leaned over to help Nancy, his longer arms reaching her.

"Bess, go after Laura!" Nancy cried.

"But—"

"I've got her," the young man said.

Bess waited long enough to make sure Nancy was going to be all right. Then she took off. Nancy's rescuer helped her climb back upward. She saw Bess's blond head bobbing through the crowd in a direct line behind Laura's dark one.

"Thanks," Nancy said breathlessly, barely glancing at her rescuer. She looked instead toward the clubhouse's glass doors. Evan might still be inside. Bess could take care of Laura, but it was time for her to go after Evan. He was the real murderer!

The security guard reached Nancy's side. "Are you all right, miss?" he asked in concern.

Seizing the opportunity, Nancy lifted a trembling hand to her forehead. "I could use some water," she said faintly.

He turned back to the entrance door. Quick as a flash Nancy followed him into the Skye Terrace's main seating area. Now to find Evan!

Skye Terrace wasn't too jammed. People were seated comfortably, many holding binoculars to their eyes. The race was about to begin.

Nancy spied Evan in the first row, by the front half-wall. His silvery hair was neatly combed, his suit immaculate. No one could tell from his appearance that just a few hours earlier he'd coldly left her and her friend to die in a blazing fire!

Suddenly a bell clanged, the gates crashed open, and the announcer's voice boomed, "They're off!"

Nancy jerked her gaze to the windows. The horses were pounding around the track! The Kentucky Derby was on!

Sidling up behind Evan, Nancy thought fast. Should she grab him? Confront him? Make a scene?

"The horses are approaching the turn," the announcer called excitedly. "It's Flash O'Lightnin' out front, followed closely by Pied Piper and Toot Sweet. . . . "

Nancy's heart hammered with excitement. She wished she had some way to keep Evan Johnson from taking off as soon as he saw her. If only she'd waited for Lieutenant Masterson's help!

"Now entering the backstretch, it's a three-horse race, folks! Flash O'Lightnin' has increased his lead to four lengths. Toot Sweet and Pied Piper are neck and neck. The rest of the field follows in this order. . . . "

Nancy closed her ears. This was the moment to grab Evan, while he was distracted by the race.

A gasp surged from the crowd. The announcer's voice yelled even louder. "Wait! Flash O'Lightnin' is falling behind in the homestretch! He's losing ground. Toot Sweet and Pied Piper have caught him!"

Nancy couldn't help glancing down to the race below. Toot Sweet, the filly of the decade, was making her bid! Pied Piper was pacing her exactly. They swept down the last furlong as one, but with a final burst of speed Toot Sweet swept under the wire first.

The crowd was on its feet, shrieking with excitement. Nancy's eyes searched the remaining horses still thundering toward the finish line. Flash O'Lightnin' had run out of gas completely. The grueling last quarter mile had finished him. He had come in tenth.

Nancy found herself screaming with the rest of the crowd, thrilled that Pied Piper had managed second place. Evan Johnson chose that very moment to glance behind him. His face contorted with the shock of seeing her there.

Nancy's gaze met him squarely. "It's over," she told him above the noise of the crowds. "The police are everywhere—looking for you."

He glanced beyond her and his face turned gray. The security guard was purposefully heading their way, and just behind him strode two of Lieutenant Masterson's men.

Evan Johnson searched for an escape but Nancy grabbed on to his arm and held him back. The police surrounded him.

Drawing a breath through his teeth, he said in disgust, "You're right, Ms. Drew. It is over."

It was dark and the Derby crowds had almost completely gone by the time Nancy, Bess, Cam, Thea, and Walt managed to meet in the clubhouse restaurant to hash over the case.

"Tell us everything, Nancy!" Thea pleaded, pulling her chair in closer. She, Cam, and Walt—who had recovered in time to ride the filly to victory—were still flushed with the success of both Toot Sweet and Pied Piper. The horses were back in their stalls, resting after their thrilling triumphs.

"I hardly know where to begin," Nancy said. "I guess it all came together when I realized it was Laura's earring I saw outside of Flash's barn that night," Nancy said thoughtfully. "When I figured out Laura had to be involved, the first question that came to my mind was, why? Why would she want to drug the horses?"

"And?" Cam prodded.

"Well, after seeing the state of the Johnsons' mansion, I realized Evan and Laura must be strapped for cash. They certainly weren't putting it back in the house. And knowing how they would want to keep up their social position and appearances at any cost, I figured the money must be gone."

"But how?" Walt wanted to know. "I thought they were loaded!"

"Everybody did. But something wasn't right. Remember when McHugh made that remark about Evan fixing a race?" Cam and Thea nodded. "Well, it made me wonder if Evan might be a gambler like his brother, U.J." Nancy's eyes twinkled. "It turned out he *was* a gambler!"

"How do you know?" asked Thea.

"Dollar Bill told Lieutenant Masterson. He admitted Evan bet on a lot more than just horses. Evan was into everything, from football pools to private poker games to horse racing. He owed Bill a bundle."

Bess's brow drew into a frown. "So how was McHugh involved?"

"McHugh knew about Evan's gambling debts. Another jockey had told him that he'd stiffed a horse for Evan in a race last March. Evan bet on the next best horse and ended up winning a lot of money."

"If Evan won so much money, then where did it go?" Cam asked.

"According to Dollar Bill," said Nancy, "Evan only exchanged one problem for another. As soon as he found out about the race fixing, McHugh started blackmailing Evan. He swore he'd tell racing officials if Evan didn't pay up. Even if his accusations couldn't be proven, McHugh knew Evan would never risk losing his social position by being put through the scandal."

"So that's when Evan decided to get rid of McHugh!" Bess cried, her eyes wide.

Nancy nodded. "Evan cut the girth strap, and it was Evan who gave McHugh the sedative that led to his accident. By the way, Lieutenant Masterson told me McHugh's come out of his coma."

"Just in time for the law to prosecute him for blackmail," Thea remarked sadly.

"So Laura drugged Pied Piper and Flash to make sure Toot Sweet won," Cam said with a whistle.

"But Toot Sweet was drugged, too," Thea reminded them.

"And someone wanted me out of the way, too," Walt added with a grimace.

"It was Evan who drugged you, Walt," Nancy revealed. "All the publicity surrounding the filly only added to her worth as a potential brood mare. When Evan saw how well McHugh's accident helped bring Toot Sweet to national attention, he decided to drug you, too, just to keep the filly in the news. He knew they'd get you to the hospital on time—at least he was counting on it."

"So it was Laura's shadowy figure you followed around the barns," Bess said, thinking aloud.

"That's right." Nancy nodded. "And it was Laura who hit me over the head. But it was Dollar Bill who we saw following McHugh that first night. After the girth strap incident, he didn't know what to think. He was worried the whole thing was going to blow up in his face, so he's laid low these past few days. That's why we haven't seen him around."

Thea sighed, leaning her head on Cam's shoulder. "At least they're all in custody now," she said with relief.

"I feel kind of sorry for Laura, though," Bess said. "She was a victim in all of this."

"Oh, I wouldn't shed too many tears," Cam remarked. "She did drug the horses, after all, and before Lieutenant Masterson took her away, she made sure I knew she was interested in me only because U.J. left me the horses. All she ever wanted was money!"

There was silence at the table as they considered everything that had happened.

Bess exhaled heavily. "I'm just glad it's all over. I don't want to have to think about anything more except having fun now. We've got one last night in Louisville. Let's make the most of it!"

Cam, Thea, Walt, and Nancy agreed heartily.

"But first I've got to call my father," said Nancy. "I know he's dying to hear all the details about the race."

Bess dimpled. "When he sent you down here he had no idea you'd run straight into a mystery."

"That's right. He was just trying to help me get over my boredom." Nancy laughed at the irony of it all. "And it worked! I've never been so unbored in my life. The Kentucky Derby *is* the greatest two minutes in sports—and a whole lot more!"

Nancy's next case:

Nancy and Ned are off to Southern California to visit Josh Kline and his younger sister, Rachel. But when Rachel disappears from her high school commencement, Nancy learns that the girl has graduated into an ultra-rich, ultra-chic, ultra-dangerous L.A. scene.

One of the guys Rachel's been hanging out with has a taste for hot cars and a distaste for all the rules. He's a prime suspect in a wave of burglaries in the Hollywood hills, but a secret society calling itself the Kats warns Nancy off the case. Rachel's been playing with fire, and Nancy knows she has to find out what makes the Kat clique tick before Josh's little sister gets burned . . . in *FLIRTING WITH DANGER*, Case #47 in the Nancy Drew Files™.